D1800104

Marsupial

Our Mother for the Time Being

Derek White

Marsupial: Our Mother for the Time Being

Copyright © 1997-2008 by Derek White
All Rights Reserved

ISBN-13: 978-0-9798080-4-3
ISBN-10: 0-9798080-4-9

Excerpts from Marsupial appeared in *Denver Quarterly*, *No Colony*, *Café Irreal*, *Harp & Altar*, *Fourteen Hills* and *Vestal Review*. Thanks go to these editors.

Printed on FSC-certified recycled paper, 30% PCW.

Published by Calamari Press
New York, NY
www.calamaripress.com

For Kevin.

"My mother is a fish."
—William Faulkner, *As I Lay Dying*

Fear of Being Asleep

There's a procession scene in it, Troy told me, before he was written off. "A scene where the vulva bed folds in on itself and you are trapped inside. In a coma of sorts." He demonstrated with his hands, forming the inside of a church we made when we were younger. "You can play that part. Our cast of degenerate pigs will carry you along in utter darkness. They'll take care of you. You won't *really* be in a coma or dead, but *actually*, you will—you can make whatever you want of it. This is your truth. You'll be comfortable, and you'll be compensated accordingly. I'll see to it."

"Why does anybody need to be in the coffin to begin with?" I asked. Marie-Yves had the logical answer, her role on the set being Continuity. You'd be able to tell by the pattern of sweat staining the shoulders of the pallbearers. The strain on their faces showing real exertion, carrying the weight of an actual human body in the black vulva coffin, along with the knowledge of it. "I'm not scripted to pop out and dance like a stripper from a birthday cake. Why don't they carry the same weight worth of something else? Sand bags? Dead fish?"

Leave it to Troy, his hands now curled back in claw formation, to turn the question back on me "You should be grateful. What if you never had the opportunity to be in the vulva bed to begin with? Then you'd never be born. And you'd never beget."

"On film," I said.

"You'd be optioned but never made. Your existence would be hypothetical." He lifted a bowl of coffee to his lips with his clawed hands, blew off some steam and took a sip, shaking his head. "We never were into the same things."

Before this scene even had a chance to happen, I was worried about falling asleep. My mind was preoccupied with the prospect of dozing off on the job when I needed to be conscious of being dead or comatose, all while being carried along in the procession. Would I be able to connect the before and after of that lost gap of time? How would I know I was the same person afterwards? I had the same healthy fear of being operated upon. I'll take being diseased over a disjointed gap in my space-time sequence any day.

In this event, it was all scripted. And I would be entombed in a black box so there would be no one but myself to verify this discontinuity. But still. It was the idea of it that preceded the act.

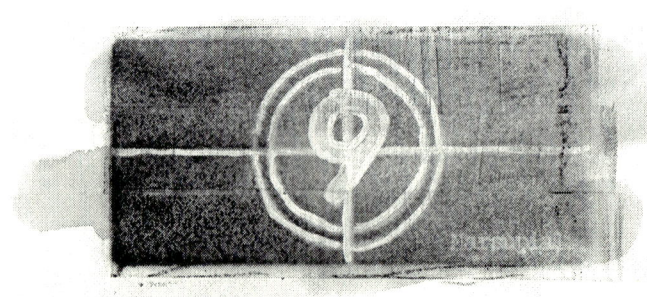

"I" Awake on the Conch-Couch (within a War Film)

The first light penetrates the living room, illuminating my brother's girlfriend's interior decoration job. A second light particle impinges, ricocheting around this foreign chamber. I am no longer in Savannah. This is all I can ascertain, even after pretending to sleep in the dark last night, in a room foreign and unfamiliar. Here is the part where I would log my dream, but the only evidence scrawled in the night was:

I was late getting to the rehearsal for a war, ad infinitum.

I'm not certain what I meant by it. I had twenty minutes to get to a "rehearsal for a war" and I didn't even know where or to whom I was supposed to report. I was assuming the war would take place on a battlefield. Waterloo came to mind, but I might have made that up to have a word to attach to the battlefield. For that matter, it was the words—"I was late getting to the rehearsal for a war"—that kept scrolling by, not the actual act of being tardy for a war rehearsal. I'm not even sure what a rehearsal for a war is. Maybe some sort of re-enactment before the fact. The mood of it resembled a wedding rehearsal. And come to think of it, the rehearsal was scheduled to be in Notre Dame.

My sentence kept repeating, over and over, all to the sound of a clock ticking and an hourly cuckoo—there was always twenty minutes to get to the rehearsal for a war. I was perpetually preparing for this sentence—reloading and checking my gun, polishing my saber, buffing my shoes—but the sentence never materialized. Then again, I didn't sleep so I'm not sure how I could have dreamt this. Now that I'm awake, I can't be certain of anything except this: My older brother John is an actor that summoned me to be his stand-in/double in a cinematic production with the working title *Crawdaddy-O & the Heroine Heir to Notre Dame*.

This pretense of sleep took place on his girlfriend Marie-Yves's conch-shaped couch. I'm not making this up—this is how John referred to it before I had even set eyes upon it, using it as a selling point to get me to come. "My hot French girlfriend has this conch-shaped couch for you to sleep on that is an actual prop from the movie we're working on. Before they killed the flesh-colored conch-couch in favor of the more refined black velvet vulva bed. You'll see." He kept saying that, "you'll see." And now I was seeing.

The material of the flannel shirt I'm wearing looks like it was cut from the same cloth as these half-ass sheets that barely cover the conch-couch. I can't tell what's what, especially sleeping on sheets that are five feet long when I'm 6'2". Even for John, who the bed was built for, it's short. He's 5'9". Which might make you wonder how I can be a stand-in for him. You might wonder why I'm documenting all this to begin with. Maybe you think it's vain. Why does this guy from Georgia think he's so important? Why does he deserve my time? Those are the very questions I've always asked myself. While I haven't found incriminating proof, I've had a sense all along about this conspiracy that everyone is in on except me. Even my brother and Marie-Yves are in on it. He might be the star of this movie, but I'm cognizant that this is really all a vast production to keep tabs on me. Standing in for him is just a distraction. It's all to establish an alibi. The second I'm out of sight or sleeping, like now, you all convene and compare notes. For what purpose? You tell me.

Staring into the darkness of these foreign surroundings, on my first night in Paris, I try to make sense of this Marie-Yves Curie, who I'm already in love with. The idea of anyway—I haven't even laid eyes on her. I'm going on the way John says her name and the fact that she's foreign and my brother's first fuck. That he's bothered to mention. You'd think with his fame would come more. The first shafts of light are slipping between these mustard curtains and I'm trying to make sense of Marie-Y by the décor of her "habitation," as John calls it. This habitation is the first I've seen of Paris by daylight. For that matter, it's the first dwelling I've slept in that belongs to a woman other than our mother.

The dissolving blackness goes unnoticed unless I close my eyes for a few moments to reference the change. A shaft refracts through a warped pane of glass and stabs me dead in the eye, inducing me to sneeze. I'm allergic to light, at least when I'm first getting used to it. Light here must be the same as it is back home. It sets off a battle with my immune system. Bodies of water trigger the same response, when I'm first getting into them, in the bath or swimming pool. People say it's the chlorine, but it happens when I immerse myself in lakes or even the ocean. Swamps I'm okay with. I'm used to them.

8

I suppress the sneeze despite warnings that it kills brain cells. What they don't tell you is that living kills brain cells. Normally, when I'm in my own element, I derive great satisfaction from sneezing out loud. But when it's this quiet and I am this unsure of my surroundings I don't want to attract attention to myself. On the third sneeze my head comes clean off, then quickly shrivels and evaporates in the sunlight like cotton candy on a wet tongue. To clarify, it's *the shell* of my head that comes off. The core remains intact. When this happens, it's just a superficial layer that is already dead. Like the exoskeleton of a molting bug. It doesn't hurt. And it all happens so fast that no one else notices, so I can't prove that it happens for real. It's just something I sense.

What's left of my refreshed mind stirs to attention, as do the molecules in the air. It's all coming back to me—my older brother will be a crawdad. He said so himself. And I am going to be his stand-in, though I am not entirely sure what this entails. That's what this is all about—why I'm here. I wiggle my toes to see if they're there and something pounces on them. I crane my neck to see—an orange cat, a rather fat one with tear-duct markings like a cheetah. I'm scared at first before I remind myself it's just a house cat and I'm a human. Sometimes I have to remind myself of my place. A cat is a cat, even if I don't know the word for it in French. I swipe my leg beneath the sheet and knock the cat on the floor next to a drain. I'm noticing now that there are a few drains on the floor, even though the floor is carpeted. The carpet is a felt material that is itchy on the feet. Maybe it's waterproof and the drains are for hosing the room down. Or maybe it's in case of floods, though we are five flights up. The cat jumps back on the conch-couch, purring. I swipe my leg beneath the sheet and knock the cat back on the floor. I suspect there are microphones or some sort of recording device in the drains, but why would they make it so obvious? Maybe it's a diversion. If I suspect I'm being monitored, that would be the obvious place I would look. The cat jumps back on the conch-couch, purring even louder. I knock the cat off again. This happens over and over until the cat is smart enough to jump over and settle in the space between my legs. I'm too tired to care about the cat or check on the drains.

My wristwatch is next to my wallet—the only familiar objects in the room. They are lying next to a few used syringes and a ruffled script. My suitcase is in a closet somewhere and my pants are on the floor, but right now I can't see them so they don't exist. I have an unhealthy fear of pants that aren't being worn that probably stems from being on the receiving end of John's hand-me-downs. Once my pants are on I'm fine, it's just when they aren't being worn—when they are laying crumpled on a floor or hanging in a closet. Gives me hives just thinking about it. In the mornings I have to reach for and put my pants on with eyes closed. John and Marie-Y don't exist either. Maybe Marie-Yves Curie does by virtue of the things in her habitation. John exists through collected memories and our shared genetics. We share the same mother: *Mary X. White.*

Going off just her name, it's only natural that I project Marie-Yves into the immediate surroundings of her habitation. There's the cat, and a pigeon roosting on the balcony. There are some torso/boat-shaped objects mounted on the wall. I asked John about them the night before and he said they were discarded prototypes of what would be his girlfriend-heroine, "towards the end of the film when things start to get dicey. It won't make sense until you've read the script." Each "torso boat" is 31 inches high, to match John, and at the bottom, in the stern, are 5 finger holes that look like they came from a bowling ball. These holes were sized to John's hand, "to keep me human, to keep my hand from turning back into a claw. This will all make sense later, you'll see." Not that it even needs to make sense. I'm just standing in for him, not acting the part.

Squinting to read in the dim light, I grab the shuffled script off the table. The title is *Crawdaddy-O & the Heroine Heir to Notre Dame.* Beneath the title is a handwritten note:

> *Dear Œuf,*
> *I' il tell yous what this est not. A waurre film.*
> *If est not rouling, no existes.*
> *B*

On the next page are "distribution instructions" that all theatres showing *Crawdaddy-O & the Heroine Heir to Notre Dame* must strictly comply to: Before the "beginning of projection," the lights in the theatre must be gradually dimmed over a period of no less than ten minutes so that the transition to total darkness is imperceptible to the open eye.

On the next page begins the actual script…

Act I: Scene i
Between Paris and Troy

EXT. Day. Plane over the Atlantic.

Opening credits dissolve in and out, superimposed on
time-lapsed nebular images.

> Dissolve to:

TROY, a disheveled 22-year old American screenwriter,
steps into a cramped airplane lavatory, slides the
lock to the OCCUPIED position. He whips out a small
black toiletry kit, removes the contents and lays
them out on the counter: A hypodermic needle, a vial
of brown granular powder, matches and a spoon (all
while superimposed credits continue to dissolve in
and out).

> Flash on:

Wing of the plane. Clouds. To the sound of jet
engines.

> Cut to:

Lighter lighting. Cooking of heroin in spoon.

> Flash on:

Aerial view of distant waves on the Atlantic Ocean.
Glimmering. Undulating.

> Cut To:

Loading of the needle, squirting off excess to void
air bubbles, etc.

> Flash on:

More swirling time-lapsed white clouds. Refracted
sunrays impinging. Perhaps in slow motion or still
frames.

> Cut to:

Troy takes off his belt. Wraps off of his arm and
thumps a vein with the finger of his opposite hand. A
needle penetrates his arm, etc. (THE TYPICAL CLICHÉS,

*Close up on arm w/ tatto

THOUGH THE ACTOR CAN FEEL FREE TO IMPROVISE TO APPEAR
MORE GENUINE.)

Zoom to:

Surface of water. The wind blows over the ocean and
stirs the surface. Visible effects of the invisible
manifest themselves. Zoom further to the body of
Troy, floating on the surface, face up, smiling.

Cut to:

Plane console with FASTEN SEAT BELT lit up. Below it
is an unlit sign that reads USE BOTTOM SEAT CUSHION
AS FLOATATION DEVICE.

Cut to:

Troy dumps the paraphernalia into the toilet and
flushes it down.

Zoom on:

Stainless steel toilet bowl with swirling blue
liquid.

Flash, split-second:

Red crawdad in toilet bowl.

Back to scene:

Troy blinks, shakes his head, looks again. The needle
is stuck sideways.

Cut to:

Troy, mildly annoyed, reaches in and slots the needle
through the hole.

Close on:

Needle being sucked through with loud suction noise.
P.O.V. of camera travels through toilet hole, into
tank and is ejected out of airplane, falling through
the clouds, spiraling.

Cut to:

Crayfish flying through the air. The camera tracks
the falling crayfish. More credits roll. Crayfish

hits the surface of the water, floats momentarily, then its tail kicks, propelling the crayfish backward into the open water, deeper into blue. Rest of credits roll, followed by the text:

THE JUDGMENT
INNER TRUTH. PIGS AND FISHES.
IT FURTHERS ONE TO CROSS THE GREAT WATER.
PERSEVERANCE FURTHERS.
            —*I CHING*

Kên

Chên

                                    Cut to:

Troy washes the blue liquid off his hands. Puts his belt back on then reaches into his pants to adjust himself. He winces and retracts his hand like he was pinched. Uncocks lock, changing it from red OCCUPIED to green VACANT.

Based on 中孚

— "The center has substance."
— the place of honor is necessary for the undertaking.
— One makes use of the hollow of a wooden boat.

3

Drapes the Same Color as Her Carpet

My head slips off my hand and I catch myself from falling asleep. This is my first morning and Paris is already a parody of itself. A church bell rings in the distance. Maybe it's been going on this whole time and I'm just now realizing it. I look out on the balcony. A pigeon circles and relocates on a weathered gargoyle just out of sight. It wasn't the noise last night—the car alarms, the sirens, people stumbling home drunk in French—that kept me awake, but the silence in between. The silence coming from the door behind which John and Marie-Yves slept. Marie-Y was already asleep when John and I got back from the airport. I heard her get up to use the toilet once in the night. I'd never heard a woman use the toilet before. It was loud and hissy. I tried but couldn't visualize what she was doing. I didn't have a face to put to it, and the extent of the visual cues John had given me was that she was a "platypus," a "ripe piglet ready for plucking," only he wished her breasts were bigger. Then Marie-Y flushed, which, like everything else around here, came off as freakish and exaggerated, something whooping and bursting. Then the patter of bare feet and the bedroom door's closure, followed by the sound of my own breathing and the high-pitch ringing in my ears, the consequence of jet lag settling in. Not that I know what jet lag is as I've never been overseas. The furthest I've been before this was to Los Angeles for a screening for one of John's other movies. And now here I am, in Paris. All because my brother's assistant called me up last week to ask me to be his stand-in. "This is a free opportunity to come to Paris. To spend time with your brother," justified John's assistant with a British accent. His "personal assistant," if you can believe it. Her name was Élodée and she sounded cute over the phone.

When I finally got this Élodée to put him on I told John he always had a way of making me feel blessed to be in his presence. He laughed and said, "do you want to come out here or not?" He said some other things while I tried to find excuses—that it was only temporary, that it wouldn't kill me, that I'd make it home in one piece. I'll admit that it crossed my mind to ask for our mother's permission. Before I realized she was dead. And that I wasn't a minor anymore. And here I am, so you know the outcome. I am not sleeping in a black box with a vial of poison and a hammer.[1]

One by one the light particles accumulate in this living room, buzzing wasps painting an impressionistic scene, shedding light on Marie-Yves's dysfunctional furniture, for the most part discarded movie props. I could be anywhere, but here I am in this living room, this "habitation," this building, on this street, in this city, in this foreign country—a country I have only read about in magazines or books or seen in movies. And my brother is a crawdad junkie and I am slated to be his stand-in. I struggle to make sense of all this, and to make sense of Marie-Yves Curie by her décor and dysfunctional furniture props. And to make sense of my brother by his choice in her. I continue reading into it.

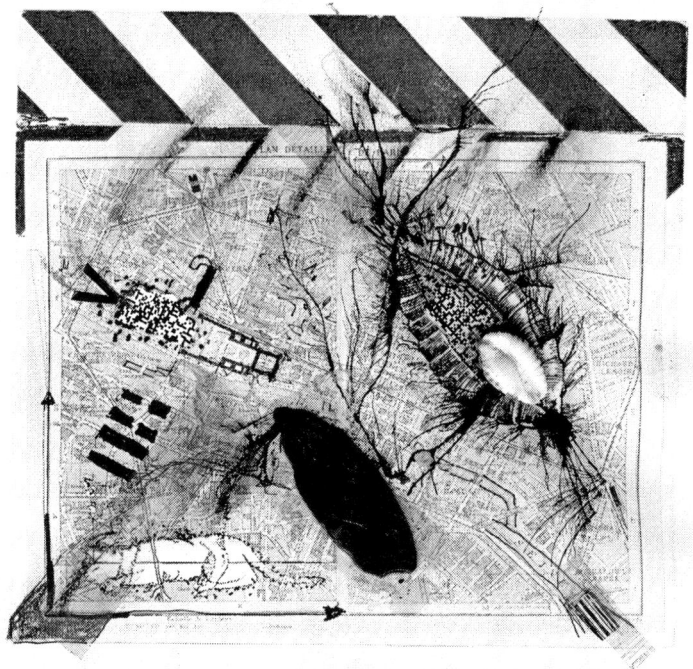

---

[1] And to think that after all this, in retrospect, John's out of the picture so to speak… but I'm getting ahead of myself.

Act I: Scene ii
Troy Needs Sustenance

INT. Day. Hotel Room in Paris.

Focus on:

Back of door. The sound of keys scraping in the lock.
The door opens and a PORTLY BELLBOY comes in lugging
a suitcase. Behind him follows Troy. He is disheveled
and unshaven, shouldering a black leather satchel.
His bright red hair is greasy and unkempt. Handheld
camera follows them into a modest room.

The portly bellboy puts his suitcase down and turns
on the light in the bathroom. He says stuff in French
(IMPROVISED, NOT SUBTITLED), which we presume Troy
does not understand. Troy tips him an American dollar
and the bellboy exits. Troy chain-locks the door from
the inside.

The camera tracks Troy as he lays down on the bed,
his legs crossed and his hands behind his head,
closing in on his face staring upward. He itches
himself. Relaxes.

Insert:

Time-lapse shot of overhead fan.

Close on:

Troy closing his eyes. They flutter in REM for a few
seconds then pop open wide.

Cut to:

Troy jumping up and pulling his laptop out of his
satchel. He pushes aside a room service menu and sets
the laptop down. As an afterthought, he picks up the
menu and glances through it.

Insert, close-up on menu:

1. PIG HIP IN GREENE CREAME SAUCE.
2. PIG KNUCKEL IN SALTE CREAME SAUCE.
3. PIG FRUITION IN HED SAUCE.
4. SAUSAGE OF PIG IN YOLKY SAUCE.
5. BOIL'D CREYFISH*.

4

Troy picks up the phone and dials two numbers.

> TELEPHONE VOICE #1
> *(overly cheerful)*
Bonjour.

> TROY
> *(annoyingly American)*
Um, yah, I'd like to get some food.

·Telephone voice #1 is no longer cheerful but goes on in ridiculously fast and incomprehensible French (IMPROV).

> TROY
> *(interrupting)*
You know—sustenance, something to tie me over, nourishment . . . (he fumbles for a pocket dictionary, drops the receiver) . . . *mangé. Yo no parlez-vous Français avec moi.*

> TELEPHONE VOICE #2
> *(in English)*
Yes monsieur? What would you like to order?

> TROY
I'll try the crayfish. Number 5. Cinq.

> TELEPHONE VOICE #2
Which habitation?

Troy rifles through his pockets for his key, drops receiver, and wedges the phone back between his chin and shoulder. The number is not on the key.

> TROY
Room . . . hold on a second.

Troy drags the phone across the floor but can't reach the door so he sets the receiver down. He yanks open the door, startling the portly bellboy on the other side with his ear pressed against it. The bellboy jumps, squeals something in French.[2]

---

[2] SPFX: For a split second, the bellboy's face morph's into a pig, as seen by Troy.

                              TROY
          Oh, bonjour. You scared the shit of me.
          Do you know what room I'm in?

                            BELLBOY
                          (perplexed)
          Room one nineteen, monsieur.

Troy thanks him, shuts the door and crawls back to
the phone.

                              TROY
          Room one nineteen. Un un neuf.

Troy hangs up the telephone. He sits on the floor for
a second thinking, then checks the door. The bellboy
is not there. He fumbles in his satchel and pulls out
paper and pens. He lays these all out on the desk
next to his laptop in an orderly fashion. He pulls
out an adapter and plugs one end into the back of his
computer. Then scans the wall for an outlet.

                                     Extreme close up on:

A European style 220-volt female outlet.

                                     Extreme close up on:

American style 110-volt male adapter. The prongs are
shaped differently and there are three holes instead
of two.

                                               Cut to:

Troy, noticeably baffled and irritated. He tries
unsuccessfully to stick the male American plug into
the female European socket. He unplugs the television
and examines the male European plug. He searches
frantically for the right outlet, moving furniture.
He throws a pillow at the television and plops down
on the bed, his head between his hands. He itches
himself. Beat. Itches himself again. His body, where
it is touching the bed, is suddenly very itchy. Troy
jumps up to examine the bed.

                                     Extreme zoom on:

Macroscopic images of bed bugs and lice. Sound of a
knock on the door.

Back of chain-locked door. Troy jumps across the room, tripping over a lamp chord, and opens the door as far as the chain will let him. There is a buxom FRENCH MAID at the door with a steaming tray of boiled crayfish. She is wearing a white apron and a black dress that pushes her breasts up.

> FRENCH MAID
> (staring past Troy suspiciously)
> ¡Bonjour! Quarante euro, si vous plait.

Extreme close on:

Maid's cleavage.

Cut to:

Troy's eyes divert from her cleavage. He closes the door and unchains it, then opens it wide. He pulls out a wad of euros of different denominations and starts handing her different ones.

The maid reaches into the wad and extracts two twenties. She remains standing with the tray of crayfish. Troy points to the desk and hustles over to clear a spot next to his laptop. She comes into the room and sets the tray down.

Insert:

As the maid leans over to set the tray down, we glimpse past the tops of her stockings and get a flash of her red garter belt. On her thigh is a tattoo of a black widow.

> TROY
> (handing her five more)
> Here. Take a little something for
> yourself.

She takes the bills and stuffs them into her brassiere and readjusts herself.

> TROY
> (visibly nervous, itching himself)
> Do you know if there's an outlet where
> I can plug in my computer?

                    FRENCH MAID
          Désolé. Je ne parlais pas Anglais.

                       TROY
            *(pointing to the European socket and
               his American plug laying on the
                      floor next to it)*
          I – need – a – jack. – An – outlet.

With his forefinger and thumb, Troy makes a hole. He
frees up his other hand and slides three fingers in
and out of the hole.

                       TROY
                (slowly, deliberately)
          Do you have – an outlet – that would
          fit – my plug?

                    FRENCH MAID
                     (blushing)
          Désolé. Moi je ne peux pas le faire.

                       Troy
          Ok. How about this.
                  *(points to the bed,
               itches his body all over)*
          Bed bugs. This bed has bed bugs.

                    FRENCH MAID
          Je ne pourrais aider a vous.

The maid reaches into her pocket and pulls out a
business card. She hands it to Troy and exits.

                                           Cut to:

Troy peeling a crayfish and eating it. He licks off
his fingers then picks up the card and looks at it.

                                         Flash on:

Card reads, "MADEMOISELLE ARAIGNÉE—ESCORT" followed
by illegible archaic script in French. At the bottom
it says "ENGLISH SPOKEN".

Troy picks up another crayfish and peels it.

BACK TO SCENE

                          8

Marie-Yves Curie Sounds the Siren

An alarm sounds from behind the closed bedroom door followed by "¡merde!" in a gravelly voice, presumably this Marie-Yves that I've heard about. My head is resting on my cocked hand, reading the script. Or sleeping. My wrist is definitely asleep, numb and itchy. Shaking it out, I put the script back on the coffee table.[3] Marie-Y's cat is still between my legs, beneath the sheet. I pretend to sleep, but the sun is right in my eyes. When I pull the flannel sheet to cover my face, my feet and the cat are exposed. This is followed by the realization that I'm hard and have oozed some on the sheet. Is this a symptom of jet lag? Or did the French maid in the script have this effect on me?

As I mentioned, I'm aware that somebody is observing me at all times. Still, I like to at least pretend to have moments of privacy or anonymity. Lying on my back, there's not much covering the outline of my leaking hard-on, so I roll over on my side. But it's not easy to roll over on this conch-couch. The door opens as I'm getting myself adjusted and in comes Marie-Yves rubbing her eyes. Through squinted eyelashes, I spy on her, breathing heavily and steadily to give the appearance of sleep. She is clad only in skimpy yellow underwear with worn elastic that rides low on her bony hips and a white baby-T hanging like a skirt above her belly button, which looks more like a slit than a button, like a horizontal caesarian section, though as far as I know she hasn't had any children. Perhaps it is a scar from a hysterectomy, though she seems young for that. Her belly is orange though the rest of her skin is white. She looks tired and vulnerable. But hers is a homely and haggard look that evokes pity. She's definitely not as foxy as John built her up to be, at least by Georgian standards.

Her routine appears unchanged despite my presence. Her acting, like she is unaware of me, is pretty good. I'll grant her that. I'm guessing she is a lead investigator of my surveillance. She might even try to get to know me intimately. It's one thing to play a minor role in my surveillance as an extra on the street, but Marie-Y has probably studied my file backwards and forwards.

---

[3] A faux pirate ship hatch from the French movie, *Perroquet, Perroquet.*

And here she is, going through this rigmarole pretending she's oblivious.

I am self-conscious of my heavy breathing—of how that must sound—so I feign a waking yawn. Marie-Y makes no attempt to cover herself. She is so skinny there is a gap between her artificially orange belly and the worn elastic of her underwear. "I see my pussy your meet," she says motioning to the cat purring between my legs.

"Back home we say cat," I respond.

"She likes you."

"Only because I don't like her, cats in general that is." I start to explain my theory about cats, but stop myself as it wouldn't make sense. My skin flushes.

Besides her orange belly, Marie-Yves's taut skin has the texture of soft eggshell or boiled shellfish—so pallid it is translucent. The faint outlines of spider veins pulse in her temples and neck. She catches me taking her in and says, "¿Ce va?"

"Say what?"

"¿Ce va?" She runs her bony hand through her short hair like she is used to having it long. It is cropped short and unkempt, whorling into her temples and forehead. She is still expecting an answer from me. "Like, how does it go?"

"Fine," I say.

"Just you say 'ce va' back, like 'it goes'."

My eyes are fixed to her eyes, afraid to drift down her body. Her eyes are dark and lackluster. What John sees in her is beyond me. All that matters to me is the idea of her. Come to think of it, she looks like photos I've seen of our mother.

Marie-Y sizes me up, exposed on the conch-couch. "How do you sleep?"

"Good," I lie.

"I hear about you a lot."

Looking past her, there's a detached cockpit from some sort of warplane I hadn't noticed the night before. Maybe sleeping in the same room as a cockpit prop is what made me dream I was late for a war rehearsal. "Oh yah? I can't imagine my brother would have a lot to say about me."

"He says only the good things. You want a coffee?"

"Oui," I say.

"Hey! You know French!"

Warmth continues to radiate into my cheeks and forehead. I must be red. I'm on the verge of some transformation. I'm disconnecting from my previous state, in a different space-time.

Luckily Marie-Y steps into the kitchen. I can still see her from behind, puttering about. Something about her posture and the lethargic way she carries herself is pathetic, but at the same time it seems natural and energy-conserving for her. My mind is occupied with what she must think of me. I need to win her over. John said I needed to get on her good side if I wanted to crash on her conch-couch. I take advantage of her being out of sight to grope around for my pants with eyes closed. I half-expect them to have wandered off and consider opening my eyes to check before I find my pants on the floor.

Marie-Y re-emerges just as I'm getting myself zipped in and opening my eyes. "We wait for the water to be hot," she says, fumbling around on the coffee table for her cigarettes. She grabs a glossy magazine and flops into a chair.[4] Her legs are folded up, exposing a banana-shaped sliver of underweared crotch lined with wisping pubic hair. I don't show it, but this is a first for me — seeing a woman expose herself so naturally. Flipping through her magazine, she stops on a photo of a gorilla petting a cat, "this is funny, you know, something about, how do you say not monkey but bigger?" She eyes me over the top of the magazine, sucking on her cigarette.

"Gorilla?" I answer.

"You are wet!" she says. "Are you hot?" I run my hand across my forehead, verifying that it is indeed layered in sweat. Marie-Y throws the magazine aside and jumps up to open the door going out on to the balcony. "I forget Americans like it cold."

"I'm okay," I say. "It's just stuffy in here is all." I don't know her well enough to explain my condition, though she probably knows about it already. After all, my condition is related to her and everyone else that is observing me. It causes me to leak from my pores when I'm conscious of this. It's my unconscious sign to them, not that I can control it. And if I did acknowledge it, it would only make it worse. My discomfort makes her uncomfortable. Searching for a distraction, I ask her about the detached cockpit prop in her living room.

"*Cock pit?*" she says. "Like a pit, a hole, for a cock? As in rooster cock or man cock?"

"I never thought of it that way," I say. "I think it's as in 'cock a trigger,' like of a gun."

"Did you want in it to sit?"

---

[4] A radar dish, not to scale, from *Les Hommes Morts Allument L'Espace Extra-Atmosphérique.*

"No thanks. I was just wondering about it." She tries to tell me what movie it was from and how they used it for insert shots with a fake sky backdrop, and the famous actors that sat in it, but these are not the details I'm interested in. I want to know what it is doing in her living room. "If an alien came from outer space that knew nothing about humans and movies, how would you explain the presence of all this?"

"Two people in it can sit," she says. "Aliens too."

"But it can't be comfortable. You wouldn't be facing each other."

"Is perfect for the watching of tele. Especial when it is a war film watching. In this cockpit you feel a piece of it. You will see why if only you try. I do it in with you."

"Not now," I say. "I'm still waking up."

She reaches around on the ship-hatch coffee table for a syringe and a vial. She pokes the syringe into the vial and extracts the liquid. Then she jabs the needle into her arm. I act like I see this every day. "This is sucks," she says. "This fucking thing."

"What is it?"

"Diabetes."

"That does suck."

"Your brother he cannot see me when I do this to myself."

"It doesn't bother me."

"Were you once in a war?" she asks.

"Not exactly," I say. "I had the same upbringing as John."

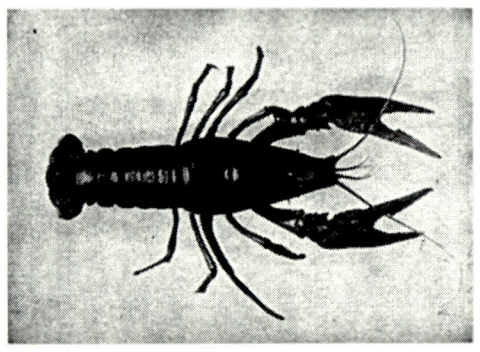

The Boiling of the Craw
Savannah, Georgia. August 12, 1983

We carried them back from the swamp in galvanized buckets. They could live out of water for hours if they had to, lethargically struggling to the top to replace those that were sinking, making clicking sounds and blowing bubbles with their mouths as they dried out. They puddled together in a bundled mass of red joints and interlocking appendages, with beady periscope eyes protruding. Once a claw got a hold of something, it wouldn't let go. Sometimes they'd grab another claw or antennae, eyes even, and pinch them off. Given time they'd grow these things back, we just never gave them a chance. We were carrying out their sentences for them.

"What do these mean," I asked John, setting my bucket down to rest my elbow.

"What do you mean what do they mean?" he asked, still holding his bucket with locked arm.

"What do they mean to us?"

"Not everything's about you. What makes you think crawdads aren't around when you're not watching?"

"You can quit your acting," I said, staring down into the bucket teeming with claws and periscopes. "I know you've been watching me all this time. Along with everyone else."

"What kind of crap is this?"

"The joke's over. You can stop your spying."

"Jesus. Who planted these paranoid ideas in your head? Your teachers?"

To be fair, they weren't teaching us evolution in school. Not that I would be opposed to it, but I was never taught it, so I wouldn't know. All I know is what I was born knowing, and what they tried teaching me about some bearded god up in the sky that up and created all this and was watching down on us. Not that I believed it, but all the kids in class went along with it, I'm thinking just to test my reaction.

"Get your head out of your ass," said John. "And lets get rolling. We don't want these crawdads dying of natural causes."

We waited with bated breath as the water boiled. We were their jurors, deliberating. Their destinies were in our hands. John was usually the one with attention deficit disorder, but he always found the patience for this act of boiling. It was me that would cave in and look. Every time John would remind me: *A watched pot never boils.*

"The pot doesn't know we're watching."

"Prove it." This was another of John's tricks when he knew he was wrong. And if it was me that questioned the validity of a statement he made, he would say, "it's possible until you can prove it's not." For instance, he would say, "a crawdad can eat the world," to which I would respond, "cannot," and he would say it was possible and I would say there was no way. And he would say just because it had never happened doesn't mean it still could.

"The water will eventually boil," I argued. "It happens every time."

"It happens when you give up watching. If you sit and watch that pot this whole time, it will never boil."

"It's boiling now."

"Only 'cause you took your eyes off it." We went through this every time. Next John would pick up a crawdad and dangle it over the pot as the crawdad clawed at the steam. He did this with every single one. He said he was doing it for them, to give them a chance to beg for mercy, but I knew he was doing it for himself. For his own mercy. They'd hit the water and turn bright red, emitting a hissing shrill. They'd struggle at first, then freeze, immortalized into sanguine statues. Poached pus would ooze from their joints and their internal flesh would become denatured. Our father said it was okay to boil them alive because they didn't have brains, just nerves. At best a nerve cluster that registered off or on, hot or cold, lightness or darkness, zero or one. When I reminded John of this, he'd say, "what does our father know? Our father who farts in heaven." To which I would say he was just mad that our father called us windbags. Sometimes John might go on to call our father a fart bag, and that we were born when he farted into our mother. To which I might say that made us fart bags. But when we were boiling the crawdads, as we got towards the bottoms of our buckets, our banter naturally died.

This act of boiling, this was nothing our father or anyone taught us. This was pure instinct. I'm not sure it ever happened, or that crawdads exist at all, or for that matter that John exists. All these things could be figments of my imagination implanted during some sort of operation. I was the one being dissected this whole time. I was the boiling pot being watched.

Nature Calling Crawdaddy-O

Smoke from her cigarette swirls into the slant of light and turns blue. The smoke she exhales is gray. Watching Marie-Yves smoke makes me nauseous. She readjusts herself, locking her knees against her chest with her arms.

"Is John still sleeping?" I ask.

"*John*?"

"My brother—John."

"Why it is you call him John?"

"Because that's his name?"

"He says for me to call him Oph." She's thumbing through a magazine indiscriminately and scratching her ankles. Her legs are long and lanky, bruised.

"That's his screen name. John is his real name."

"But why 'Oph'? What does this mean?"

"All I can tell you is that off-white is a shade of white that is not quite white. How about you? Are you related to Madame Curie, the physicist?"

Marie-Y laughs. "No. But I am great granddaughter to Albert Camus." The bedroom door swings open and John makes his grand entrance in Popeye[5] pajamas. "Good morning John!"

"John is a toilet," he says. "A depository for human waste."

"Stu says John is your name."

John sighs. He looks foreign and unfamiliar to me. I've never seen him in the presence of a "girlfriend." And I am still not used to his shaved head. The dark stubble is just starting to come in. His skin is starting to fold under his neck and he's gained weight. But he's got a tan, fresh from the weekend before in the French Riviera.

"That's the name our parental beings gave you," I say.

"That's the funny thing about birth names. They have to settle on something before they even know who you are."

The kettle whistles and Marie-Y jumps up. "Why is it your brother talk different from you, John boy?

"On account of his redneckedness," says John, mocking my accent. "And don't be calling me John Boy."

"At least I'm not denying where we're from," I say.

---

[5] Featuring a montage of scenes with Popeye sucking spinach through his pipe.

"And where's that, a swamp? Actually, if you want to get down to brass tacks, you should be calling me Crawdaddy-O."

The Proper Sense of the Word

Craw•dad (kráw´dad´) *n. sl.* chiefly southern U.S.
See *Crawfish*.

Craw•fish (kráw´fîsh´) *n.*
See *Crayfish*.

Cray•fish (krE´fîsh´) *n.* Also known as crawdads, crawdaddys, crawfish, mudbugs, jibby-jabbies and yabbie-yabbies. Any of various edible decapod crustaceans (of phylum arthropoda) found in freshwater rivers, streams, ponds (that don't freeze to the bottom) and swamps of temperate regions, with a few saltwater species. Crayfish burrow into muddy banks or under rocks and feed on animal and vegetable matter. Crayfish have been discovered underground to depths of 3 meters. Some cave-dwelling species are blind. Crayfish typically grow to 6 inches in length, but have been found up to 10 inches. Crayfish possess eight pairs of legs, the first three have been modified for feeding, the remaining five are for motion. If crayfish lose an appendage, they grow it back. The tail is also used for locomotion, with a curling action that propels the crayfish backwards. All internal organs and muscles are attached to a hard and chitinous exoskeleton. Breathing takes place through internal gills. Unprocessed material is defecated through a mud-vein. Crayfish are chiefly nocturnal. If crayfish are spotted during the day they are likely diseased (see also, *crayfish plague*). Crayfish have no brain (in the proper sense of the word), just a modified spinal cord that responds only to motor stimuli, and thus are commonly the subject of biological experimentation and vivisection. Crayfish are commonly eaten, especially in Southeastern U.S. and France.

The Toilet Dysfunction

"Why Crawdaddy-O?" I ask, gathering a change of clothes from my duffel bag.

"Don't ask me, I'm just the actor," says John. "That's a question for Bernard."

"Whose Bernard?"

"The director and writer. And flaming junkie."

My head is down low searching through my folded clothes. I catch a glimpse of my folded pants and try not to think about it, which never works. I start rising until I'm peering over the top of my hunched-over self, still down rifling through my garments. My hands reach the bottom of the bag but don't come up with anything. When "I" try to pick something up, I discover "I" have no control over my hands. On closer inspection, they are actually flesh-colored claws.

"Just settle on something already," says John. There was a time when John always told me to "never settle," so I knew he now he was caving in. "Do you need to borrow a shirt for christ sake?"

I pick something out, but I can't tell what it is as I'm hovering further up toward the ceiling. John and Marie-Yves are still looking at my body below, standing in the middle of the room. I'm holding a conversation with them, which is reassuring. I'm asking John about the script, who Troy is. He claims to be Troy. And when he takes this narcotic bug juice he transforms into Crawdaddy-O. It all sounds vaguely familiar as he is explaining. Déjà vu like a movie I've seen back home. My momentum shifts and I start to sink down to the level of my body.

"What is a crawdaddy?" asks Marie-Y. "You know, in this real world." My perspective shifts and "I" start to rise again.

"They're these spineless bugs that dwell in mud," says John, in a sarcastic voice like he is reading scripture.

"Bugs?"

"Technically that's their closest relative. They're bugs that regressed and went back into the swamps."

Marie-Y remains baffled so I take it upon myself to alleviate her confusion, or at least my body does—I am able to move his lips. They tell her that a crawdad is also known as a crayfish, and that it is like a small lobster that lives in fresh water. While this telling is going on, I watch Marie-Y who thinks she's looking at me, but Stu is not looking back. Little does she know I'm hovering right over her. I could even peak down her shirt if I want to but I fixate elsewhere.

"I don't know why your brother he does not just say it this way in the beginning."

John is on the conch-couch now, slouching and fidgeting where I was sleeping. He's surfing the channels with the volume muted. He grabs at the orange cat and pets it hard. The cat doesn't seem to mind. Then John smells something. He pushes the cat aside and sniffs at the couch. "It fucking stinks here like fish. What did you do in your sleep, Stu?"

"I" am not able to answer. I try to pinch myself but can't move my own fingers.

John dabs something off the sheet and inspects it between rubbing thumb and forefinger. "Scales," he says. "Were you cleaning fish between the sheets? You haven't changed one bit."

I want to tell him to stop pinning it on me, but when Stu's lips finally move—they say, "John and I caught them. When we were little. Remember that?"

"Caught what?" John says, still smelling his fingers. I linger closer to him, curious to know what the smell evokes, but also cautious, instinctually knowing if I get too close I will attach myself or wake up.

"Crawdads," Stu answers.

"Don't change the subject."

"It's true, we used to boil them alive."

"Leave it to Stu to remember this shit."

"I bet you never figured those experiences would come into play in your professional career?" Stu says. "Getting into character and all."

"Troy doesn't become a real crawdad," says John. "It's all a metaphor for being a junkie."

Then it was like John and Marie-Y were speaking in French. Even though I didn't know a word of French, I could understand what they were saying. And they couldn't have been speaking French because John doesn't know any. Marie-Y brings us coffee in bowls. Stu accepts it and sits down in a director's chair that says 'Chuy' on it, acting like he had been drinking coffee out of a bowl his whole life. Crossing his right leg over the other, I hear him ask, "why is the script in English if it's a French-made movie?"

"Further reach," says John.

"Who's this Troy guy?"

"You mean in the script?" says John, petting the cat and surfing the TV, stopping for no more than ten seconds on each channel. "He's a writer that never writes anything. He gets sucked into this bug culture on the pretense of writing about it. It's all pretty dumb. Just another movie about making movies. Bernard's projecting his own issues into this script to meet a deadline or quota. Film is the only reality he knows and they always teach you to write what you know. Personally, I think it's more interesting to write about what you don't know."

I'm drifting further away towards the balcony, roosting with the pigeons on the railing. My body is still standing in the middle of the living room with a change of clothes in hand—waiting for a break in the conversation to take a shower. John is surfing the channels, talking. I can't hear anything through the window. He stops on Bugs Bunny with an Acme vacuum cleaner. Bugs is vacuuming up stuff around him. He vacuums up Elmer Fudd's gun, and then Elmer Fudd, and the trees and the environment, and then himself, and then the vacuum cleaner vacuums itself up until there is nothing left but the credits rolling in French and John changes the channel.

"Let me get this straight in my head," Stu says. "You're John, who calls himself Oph, who is acting the part of Troy, who transforms into Crawdaddy-O?"

"If you have to put it that way," says John grabbing the sheet I was sleeping on, wadding it up and throwing it at Marie-Y, telling her to put some clothes on, to cover herself up, like he's just noticing now. I take this as my cue.

"Can I take a shower now?" Stu asks Marie-Y.

"What do you means, *take*?" she says. "Take where?"

"Douche," says John.

"Of course," she says. "Do you want to sit yourself in my cock pit before that of your toilet?"

"Is this required?" Stu asks, which causes John to burst out laughing, causing Stu to turn red. "I mean, is it like something you do here, a custom of some sort?"

"Is not like that," says Marie-Y.

"I'll just take that shower now," says Stu. He hesitates then enters the bathroom and closes the door. My point of view regresses back out on the balcony, watching John and Marie-Y through the window. John is still laughing about the connection between cockpits and showering and Marie-Y thinks he is laughing at her English. A third of the time he calls her platypussy, a third of the time he calls her pigpussy and a third of the time he calls her platypig. I can't hear much of what they're saying, but it sounds like arguing now. Something about the beach and girls and skin tones. I can read their lips. John laughs at Marie-Y for being so white after all the time they spent in the French Riviera. She can only get tan on her belly, and even then it's orange. She says she can't help it. That's who she is. John complains about her not having tits. Marie-Y throws a glossy magazine across the room. John lifts his arm and deftly deflects it, but it lands on the cat. The cat's had enough and saunters off and takes refuge in the cockpit prop of all places. John tells her she is making Stu uncomfortable. Her lips mouth something about underwear, but I get too wrapped up in her lips to decipher what they are saying. John is not listening but watching a French game show with three buxom blondes in referee uniforms dancing in the background behind the host. John complains that the cat has fleas. Pinches one between his fingers and presents it to Marie-Y as evidence. To an outsider, this gesture comes off as an offering. She asks how he knows it's not Stu and he laughs and says he doesn't, and they both laugh together this time. The doors of the clock swing open and the cuckoo bird makes an appearance. The pigeons next to me scatter. The cuckoo retreats, then comes back out and does it again. John and Marie-Y continue arguing, but now it's about the clock. John wants to get rid of it, but Marie-Y says it belonged to her grandfather. Their arguing escalates. John mocks the way she says "heirloom." Marie-Y springs up out of the chair-cum-radar dish, pouncing on John. He grabs her left tit and twists it through her shirt. He keeps insisting she doesn't have any, and she asks him what he is twisting. Apparently this is some sort of game they play often. It seems scripted. He insists one is bigger than the other and she lifts her shirt to examine them. Their methods are not very scientific. Then I swear I see John's hand disappear inside of her. Not down between her legs, but in some crease by her belly button where I noticed the horizontal incision. Maybe the belly button itself. She slaps his hand away and begs his forgiveness, for her imperfections, then asks what about him? She says he is shaped like a "fishing pole when something is on the line." She's fumbling around for his fly and at that point I don't feel I should be watching so I pan left to where I can zoom in on Stu taking a shower. Though he's not taking a shower. The water is running but he is standing, listening at the door. He checks the knob but it doesn't lock. I don't know what he's more afraid of, John seeing him this way or Marie-Y. John and Stu are of the same cloth, but in other ways that makes it harder. The bathroom is filthy. The light is bright. Stu cowers away from it. The "bathtub" is really a rowboat with a drain built into the bilge. Mold is proliferating between the wood slats of the hull. There is no showerhead or curtain, just two faucets in the stern. Stu turns his attention to it. He picks up a plastic scooper and examines it. He feels the water. Turns the left faucet on and twists the right off. He can't tell hot from cold. He still has his clothes on. He scratches his arm and a crust of skin flakes off. He examines it and peels off another piece that extends from his elbow to his wrist. Pus glistens beneath the molted shell. Stu is new to this. He licks his arm to taste it. Nibbles on a piece of the shell then spits it out. Dabs a washcloth in water and tries to wipe himself down, but the pus is not water-soluble. He looks in the medicine cabinet and finds what smells like rubbing alcohol. When he applies some to his arm, he swears he sees thousands of tiny red mites scattering and penetrating back into cracks in his skin. He should know because Stu is me. The rubbing alcohol dissolves the pus. Once the gooey pus is wiped clean, his arm appears no worse than irritated. Sunburnt perhaps. Still, Stu looks concerned. He picks up the pieces of his shell and considers what to do with them, finally opting for the toilet, though it appears there are two types of toilet. And a plunger in between. He picks the one that most resembles what he is used to back home—the one that holds water. He examines the pieces of shell after he drops them in the toilet. This induces him to take a crap. As he is sitting on one toilet, he turns the faucet on the other to discover it is a toilet-cum-fountain. When Stu is finished and wiping, he spots blood on the toilet paper. He has no one to share this information with, and if he did, he wouldn't. He wipes again and looks closer to find miniscule white worms. He wipes again, blotting. It's a different story every time. He's realizing that whatever he's afraid of, he'll find. He's convinced that red chigres have burrowed into his skin, deep into his gut where they are incubating, inducing this molting. Sure enough, he sees the tiny red mites on the tissue when he wipes. By this time I'm back inside him for good.

Notre Dame Lays Between Paris and Savannah
International Waters. April 2, 1981.

Our mother is lost at sea.

Mother Mary Comes

John barges into the bathroom, waking me up. I'm huddled in the moldy bath boat with the lukewarm water filling. "I got to piss like a racehorse," he says in a mock southern accent. He's urinating before he even gets the lid up. I made sure there were no molting remnants, but still, I have a nagging sense he might discover something.

"What's the story with this bath tub?" I say, trying to cover my raw arm. "Does everyone in France bathe in boats or was this from a movie?"

John looks at the tub like he's seeing it for the first time. "It works," he says, then aims back at the toilet. "Nasty burn you got there."

"I'm just noticing it myself."

"You and my platypig both."

"Yeah, I noticed her belly."

"She says she doesn't react well to these lights." He nods up toward the ceiling.

"I noticed they were kind of bright."

"I got to have them. They're artifice lights, to simulate the conditions on the set."

"Artificial lights?"

"Only naysayers call them artificial. They are artifice. Others claim they are reptilian molting lamps."

"Is that what's going on with my arm?"

"Dude, that's a pre-existing condition."

"Why do they call them molting lamps?"

"Some people claim to have adverse reactions to artifice lamps. Like Marie-Yves, she blames them for her orange belly." John finishes then flushes. "So what do you think? Besides the belly?"

"She's a good catch. For you," I say, scratching my arm. "I'm thinking what I have though, isn't a sunburn but chigres. I'm thinking I got them so bad they've become an integral part of me."

"Don't be an idiot. Chigres don't burrow into you. They spit a salivary secretion on you with digestive enzymes that liquefy your skin so they can slurp you up." He considers me scrunched in the bath boat. "Are you sure we came from the same mother?"

"You tell me."

"Watch this." John takes the plunger and dips it in the bathwater. Then he suctions it to his forehead. "This is what Pinocchio, my arch enemy, looks like." John buzzes around the room with the plunger sticking out of his head.

"Thanks for dipping that thing in my bathwater."

"You aren't supposed to fill the tub. That's a decadent American thing. Use that scooper to bail water over yourself. Or do the sponge thing. And in case you're wondering, this thing ain't for pissing." He kicks the porcelain toilet-cum-fountain with the nozzle in it.

"You think I've never seen a bodega before?"

"It's bidet, you douche bag. And it ain't for tickling your balls."

"Why are you talking like that?"

"Like what?"

"Like you're mocking me."

"You don't own the way we speak."

"I've never heard you talk like this before."

"I'm an actor. I have to turn on accents on demand."

"Yah, well, your shit still stinks."

"Speaking of your shit stinking, slap some of this on when you're through in here." John grabs a bottle from the medicine cabinet. "*Eau de toilette*," he says.

"What's that supposed to mean?"

"Toilet water."

"What's the point?"

"To purify. Jesus, you worry too much. This is all temporary. Try to enjoy yourself while you're here. But no funny stuff." He shows me the label with Virgin Mary bathed in a halo of light. "Mother Mary is watching."

N°4711. Eau de Cologne

Da più di 100 anni la marca preferita dall'alta aristocrazia

In vendita presso tutti i principali negozi del genere,

4711 Eaux de Toilette
4711 Extraits d'Odeurs
4711 Savons fins de Toilette
4711 Savons à la Glycérine
4711 Poudres, Sachets, Sels anglais

Etichetta verde e oro.

What the Reservoir Held
Gaston Sewage Treatment Center, Savannah. Circa 1980-82.

It was an island of order in the swamp we called our backyard—a pond the shape and size of an Olympic swimming pool, moated by a rectangular levee of red clay. The banks held onto their symmetry despite the summer rains that eroded ruts. This was our special place to get away from our parental beings.

Sometimes the levee was covered in protective mulch. We never witnessed who spread this matter on the banks. Within weeks the mulch would decay into the mucky clay or be swept down the banks into the containment pond where it was reabsorbed. The containment reservoir absorbed everything. Cresting the levee was a barbed-wire fence that was no obstacle for us—we simply snaked under it.

Artificial lights lined the perimeter. Machinery grinded and gurgled just over the west side of the levee. The pipework was green where it wasn't rusted through and snaked over and into the pond. There were two pipes—we assumed one was in and the other was out, but couldn't tell which was which. We never saw anyone running the pipework and machinery. The machine ran perpetually off the very matter it was processing. It smelled of dirty bleach and decay. A circular tank churned and processed a frothy liquid. We did not understand this complex machinery, but this was not what we were after. We were interested in the containment reservoir and what lived in it.

John called it our experiment with life—a re-enactment of the conditions from which we came. But the story changed every time. It was something we stumbled upon that was not meant for our eyes. It evolved as we did. It was a top-secret government conspiracy harboring alien life forms. Or we were spies undermining a plot of global genocide using nitrogen-fixing bacteria, or viruses disguised as commercial fertilizer. Or we were banished scientists flying kites with tailing keys in thunderstorms, the kite strings weighted to the reservoir with an old bicycle frame, upping the ante on Ben Franklin. We channeled the lightning into something more horrific than Frankenstein. Within the confines of the containment reservoir, our laboratory animals underwent mutations. Our frogs walked upright. We called them frogzillas. Our crawdads were huge alien monsters. Mamnewts were their formidable victims. Following Mendel's example, we seeded the cesspool for our own devices. We were the first to transplant crawdads, mamnewts and frogzillas from the swamp to the isolated pond. It was a veritable Noah's ark. We noted their traits as they thrived and multiplied exponentially. We bred mamnewts with frogzillas and frogzillas with crawdads. We shared their oxygen. When we handled them they left a slimy film on our hands that we knew our mother would scold us for. They silently fed us their knowledge and we fed them hot syrupy cola and sweaty candy. When they ran out of things to teach us, we turned them into gummy mamnewts or frogzillas and ate them. We made crusts of the red clay and turned them into pies. And they were the only eyewitnesses.

The arthropods fed on the amphibians—the spineless hunters and the gill-less hunted—in our coliseum of morbid fecundity. When the supply of mamnewts ran low, the bigger-clawed crawdads cannibalized their own. The decaying matter spurned more algae growth, which re-infused the mamnewt population. Our crawdads and mamnewts had one thing in common—they were both the color of the clay that made them. Both were rusted red from stagnation and inbreeding. Through it all they managed to survive and multiply. Until they eventually outgrew the pond—overflowing the red banks, under the barbed wire and back to the swamp where we originally got them. And we outgrew them. The eroding ecosystem of the cesspool still lives on without us, and within us.

Gradually, the containment pond became us. The rust-colored cesspool bled upwards into the hot air. Liquid and vapor were one and the same. We existed in a sultry diorama where our sweat, breath, spit, piss and blood were shared by all—by the sodden ground, the murky waters, the musky undergrowth and the stinking beasts that lurked within our isolated landscape. Our breath sublimated into the dripping Spanish moss and tangled vines. We'd drink cola and eat gummy worms while our sweat and piss rusted the barbed wire into the clay. We did it all over again, recycling our cells into one another. We were consumed by something bigger than ourselves.

When we got home, we'd tell our mother we weren't hungry and she would scold us for spoiling our appetites.

Taking Inventory of the Surroundings

The sound of the toilet flushing is replaced by the sound of the holding tank refilling. John shoves the eau de toilette with the Virgin Mary label under my nose. "Smoke this in your corncob pipe," he says.

"I ain't wearing that sissy perfume."

"It's cologne. It's androgynous."

"It smells like that stagnant cesspool we used to play at. Remember that place?"

"The sewage treatment place? Where they processed our crap?"

"We bred our crawdads there."

John shuts the medicine cabinet and examines his face in the fogging mirror. "You would remember that." He opens the door. I can see Marie-Yves through it. "We gotta get a move on, Stuey boy. We have to be at the studio by eight. And by the way, you may as well launder your clothes while you're at it. We don't have a washing machine and they don't believe in Laundromats here. Just take a bath with your clothes on—kills two birds with one stone." John exits. "I" am tempted to float out with him but remain hovering in the bathroom, looking down on Stu hunkered naked in the boat tub with his red left arm. John and Marie-Y resume their scripted arguing on the other side of the door. This time it's about her smoking.

Stu picks up the soap, attempting to reinvent his toilet ritual. I take the opportunity to inventory the contents of Marie-Yves Curie's medicine cabinet:

- Alcool de Frottage, 500 ml
- Botot, pâte dentrifice, 150 ml
- Générique Prozac, 20 mg x 30
- Vagyl, poudre antiseptique vaginal, 150 mg
- Recouvrement de poche de cellophane, 12 count
- lipstick, black
- Halcion oral (triazolam USP CIV) 10* 0.125 mg
- Cumulus Umbra tampons, 12 count
- Le serum regenerist pour les Yeux d'Olay, 50 ml

41

- Notre Dame eau de toilette, 300 ml, half empty
- Orconectes Viriles condoms, boîte 12 count, 7 remain
- gauze, 1 roll
- Men-Ü facial moisturiser après rasage hydratant
- Procambarus Clarkii nail clippers
- Q-tips
- Calamox lotion de calamine, 300 ml

Reaching from the boat, Stu grabs a dirty T-shirt and underwear off the floor. When Stu brings the clothes into the boat tub, I am back in his P.O.V. It is a strange sensation to bathe with clothes. It would be even stranger *wearing* them in the bath per John's suggestion. Ladling water over myself with a scooper is a strange enough way to bathe, especially in a vessel shaped like a rowboat. It's like basting yourself in your own juices. Every other time I've bailed water in a boat has been under the impending fear of sinking. It's hard to get past that until I stop thinking about it. I get immersed into the rhythm of the water sloshing back and forth. I find myself aroused though I can't explain it. This is the essence of arousal—not being able to explain. Arousal is a trick our bodies play to get us to do something productive we might not otherwise think to do.

Afterwards I regret it—feeling like I've been had. I wring my clothes out and change into dry ones. I apply some of the pink calamine lotion to my arm, hoping it will at least smother the chigres if they try to re-emerge. At least when somebody asks me what's wrong with my arm, I'll have a simple one-word answer: "calamine."

When I open the door to exit, Marie-Y is waiting to take my place. There is an awkward moment when neither of us knows what to say. I say, "it's all yours," wondering how that would translate word for word. She says she's sorry, that she really has to pee, and I say I'm sorry back, that I wish she had told me. She winks. I don't notice if she notices the pink lotion.

I am certain she won't arouse herself when I'm not present, though she may leave evidence of it to make me think otherwise. I take my wet clothes and drape them over the wrought-iron balcony like it's already a daily ritual for me. I settle on to the conch-couch. A call sheet lays on the coffee table hatch, next to the script.

CRAWDADDY-O & THE HEROINE HEIR TO NOTRE DAME

Call sheet
Day No. 7
1st Unit
Monday, September 23, 2005

Shooting Call:	08h00
Lunch:	13h00
Wrap:	18h00

Meeting Place: Studios de la Suture, Paris. Stage 5.

sc#	Synopsis	Set/Location	INT/EXT	D/N
45	Four sailors pummel Crawdaddy-O	Alley	EXT	N
93	Crawdaddy-O 'claws' gypsies	streets (sect 17)	EXT	D
104	Pinocchio 'stings' tourist	Metro (Eiffel st.)	INT	—
47	Spider-whore rescues Crawdaddy-O	Porkfish Belly	INT	N
96	Nuclear raid on Crawdaddy-O	Plastic Bubble	INT	—
37pt1	Troy visits Morrison's grave	Morrison gravesite	EXT	N

Roles	Makeup FX	Makeup/ Costume	Shooting Call	Sc. #
Crawdaddy-O	Crawdad costume	07h00	09h00	45,93,47,96
Sailors 1,2,3,4	Tattoos, uniforms	07h30	09h30	45
Tourist	Tourist garb	10h30	11h30	104
Pinocchio	Mosquito costume	09h30	11h30	104
Spider-whore	Spidery Costume	10h30	12h30	47

Stand-ins Troy/Crawdaddy-O (Stuart White) on set at 08h00
Pinocchio (Thierry Leroq) on set at 11h00
Spider-whore (Joan la'Orcase) on set at 12h00

Extras Gypsies: on set at 9h00
Tourists: on set at 10h30
Morrison gravesite dwellers: on set at 16h30
Metro riders: on set at 14h00
Futuristic "SWAT" team members: on set at 15h00

Function:	Time:
Director..	08h00
Director of Photography...	08h00
Assistant Directors...	08h00
Assistant Camera..	09h00
Sound...	08h15
Wardrobe..	07h00
Continuity..	07h30
Makeup FX...	07h00
Art Department..	07h00
Grips...	08h00
Lighting..	08h00
Production..	07h00
Stunt Coordinator..	08h00

Art Dept./ Set Dressing:	silk thread "spider webbing", cobwebs
	brass knuckles
	plastic isolation bubble w/ "nuclear" drawer
	tourist camera w/film
	crawdad boxer shorts
	3x syringes
	3x bottles of Jack Daniels
	variety of drug paraphernalia

```
                          casket

Special Effects:         mist
                         severe wounds (lacerations and bruises) on Crawdaddy-O
                         decapitated sailor's head and misc. body parts
                         blood splattered on dumpster/garbage soaked in blood
                         white pus
                         claw ripping through flesh
                         Pinocchio's "growing syringe" nose
                         12" hypodermic needle penetrating tourist neck
                         Crawdaddy-O "crawling" on eight legs
                         decomposed body in open casket


Costumes:                sailors
                         gypsies
                         tourists
                         gravesite dwellers
                         futuristic "nuclear" SWAT costumes


Special Equipment:       variable speed/stroboscopic fisheye
                         soft focus/filtered lenses
```

- Need a boat.
- Think "cruw"

Dotting the "i" in Heirloom

John tells me to come and get it in the same voice as our mother. Waking on the conch-couch, I answer his call without thinking. First he calls me on the pink smears of calamine lotion coating my arm, telling me, "make-up won't have it. Even if you're just a stand-in." Then he asks, "what are *we* going to do about your hair?" As a stand-in they might have to dye it to match Troy. Which really means John, once or twice removed.

The color is blood red. They'll need to bleach it first to get the color to stick. My consolation is monetary payment. John says I should be grateful, that my hair couldn't be in any worse shape than it is. And that it's only for the time being. "It's just hair," he says, "dead protein strands sprouting from the top of your head."

"I never said otherwise," I say.

He palms his head, "you can always be like me—shave your head and wear a wig. Then you can be anyone. Or no one." John folds a table down from the wall and instructs me to sit. I act like I'm used to kitchen tables that fold down from walls. I don't notice any recession on John's hairline, but there's a lump forming in the center of his forehead, right on the scalp line. "Dude. Looks like you're sprouting a horn."

He feels his forehead. "Must be the lighting."

"Let me guess, artifice?"

"Damn straight. And don't be pointing this out to anyone. Including Marie-Yves. Something as small as a zit can delay production for days."

"I figured you were growing a horn or something. I was reading how that's the thing to do in L.A."

"Where did you read that, the Savannah Mourning News? If I grew a horn, the only role I would get would be as a unicorn centaur."

"Or Satan."

"Satan has two horns." He grabs two pieces of toast from a box and throws them on my plate. "Sorry, they don't believe in toasting their toast here." I act like I eat pre-toasted toast from a box every morning. "Don't worry," he says. "Paris is not all that bad." As I attempt to spread hard butter across the stiff crumbling toast, John briefs me on all the nightclubs and cabarets of Paris, one in particular where all the girls have shaved heads. It's not just about how perfect the girls bodies are, but he stresses how well-proportioned they are as *a group*, in a line. To the point where you are not looking at individual girls, but clones of an idealized concept—a breed. "This is the intention," he says. "It's all about desiring the *idea* of 'girl' and not a particular one."

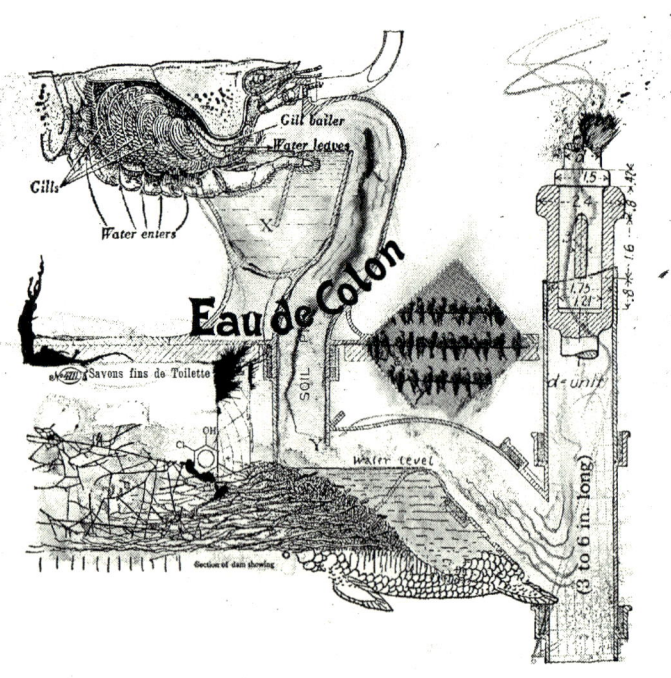

Suturing the Crevasse

Folk etymology of *Crawdad*
White Residence, Savannah, GA. January 6, 2006.

The crawdad, also known as the crawfish or crayfish, owes its name to a series of serendipitous misunderstandings. Crayfish is related etymologically, as well as biologically, to the crab. The actual source of the word is believed to be from the old French *ecrevisse* from the old Frankish *krebitja* (crab)(from the same root as crawl), or the Middle English *crevise*, first recorded in a document written in 1349 A.D. (during the Bubonic Plague). In old French and Middle English these words signified the crayfish. Before the advent of comparative etymological science and the laws underlying homophonic change, the evolution of words was often due to colloquial mutation (intentional or not). In the case of *crevise*, people began to pronounce and spell the last part of the word as if it were 'fish,' the first fish spelling (actually *fysshes*) being recorded in 1588 A.D. The reversion to craw*dad* is perhaps a matriarchal retaliation for the disjointed association of mothers with fish.

Even Crawdads Once were Bedwetters

St. Augustine, Florida. January 2, 2006. 7:17 a.m.
INT. Dream Sequence.

I woke up to relieve myself. Disoriented at first because I wasn't home, I found myself in a hotel room in Florida with our father. According to his doctor, he was supposed to be dead. We were on the first night of a weeklong father-son surfing trip. John was shooting a film so couldn't make it.

There was a crayfish in the toilet. I was conscious that I was conscious. Maybe I had already been up once before—I had been known to sleepwalk, especially when I was out of my element. I had to go bad so I peed in the sink and let the water run. It took forever to empty my bladder. By the time I was through, my eyes had adjusted to the dim light. What would we do if one of us had to take a crap? I couldn't fall back asleep, so I woke our father to tell him.

"Still wetting the bed, are we?" he said in a patient fatherly way.

"For real," I said. "See for yourself."

He got up and saw for himself. "Indeed, there's a crayfish in the toilet. This sort of thing probably happens in Florida."

"What do we do? He'll pinch us if we reach in. I'm not sure I want to reach in there anyway. And if we did get him out, then what?"

It was too late. My father flushed the toilet. "Go back to bed," I swear I heard him say.

Tonguing Her Name

Water streams down her pallid neck, translucent veins that merge and diverge. John insists she is a vampire.

"Moi?" says Marie-Yves, hand to her chest along the towel line. A blue vein pulses her in her neck.

"Yes you, my little platypussy vampire."

"¿De quoi parlent-ils?

"Sang. Le Lun," says John. "We were talking about the movie. An American junkie, yours truly, falls in love with a Parisian vixen-vampire." John grabs her ass under the towel.

"¡Arrete!" she says, slapping his hand away and reaching for her cigarettes. "I thinked she is a prostituée?"

"Troy's women wear many hats," says John, sipping his coffee. Marie-Y lights a cigarette and exhales smoke in my face. "So," says John, "Stu thinks you don't want him here."

"I didn't say that," I protest, kicking John under the table.

"It is no problem," she sighs, dangling her cigaretted arm off to the side. "My habitation is your habitation. For the being of time."

"Thanks Marie-Yves," I say. As she comes out of my mouth, I realize it's the first time I've spoken her name out loud, causing my face to flush.

"Way to butcher her name," says John. "It's Mar-ee-eaves. Breathe in on the last two syllables. Like our mother with an eves on the tail end. It helps if you smoke. French was created for smokers, to pace their exhalations with inhalations."

"Don't be a stupid," says Marie-Y, taking a drag of her cigarette and blowing smoke to the side. "This brother of yours says it just as sucks as you. You are American, you can't expect to be speaking how we French do. Hundreds of years breeding went to this tongue." She bellies up to John, drags her tongue across his forehead, then exits.

The Doubled Cone Trap
Intracoastal Waterway, GA. March 27, 1971.

"I'd hate to get my pecker stuck in there," John said. "There" was a cylinder of fine-meshed chicken-wire with the ends collapsed conically inward, doubling back to crude unhemmed holes just big enough for a crayfish to pass. On the inside we strapped a can of tuna with triangles punctured along the rim. The crayfish would smell the tuna and crawl in, dropping into the trap. Once in, it was difficult to retreat. Crayfish were adept at swimming backwards, but they couldn't steer too well.

"Rubs you the wrong way thinking about it," said John. "Their claws would get caught and wrenched back if they tried to climb out the way they went in."

He threw the trap out into the Savannah River—the river that connected to the Intracoastal Waterway that inevitably connected to the Atlantic—where our mother was last seen, though the search party had long since been called off. We had used the crawdad trap with success in the paludal inland waters, now we wanted to try it in the brackish estuary at the edge of the tide's retreat. Just off the shore of the cemetery.

The sinking trap emitted an expanding collage of rainbow oils that stained the surface of the water, then swirled into the eddies and currents of the river.

"Crawdads can smell like we see," said John. "They smell in color. With depth perception and everything."

"How can we know that?"

"I saw a special on it. There's this whole world available to them that we aren't privy to."

"Dad says what our mother had between her legs was a trap."

"That would make his pecker a crawdad then."

"I reckon it would."

While the doubled cone trap was in the water, we ate gummy worms and drank cola on her grave. We speculated about what was in the river that we couldn't see. If we couldn't catch it in our trap to bring back home, it didn't amount to anything.

Inquisition of a Platypusdad

"How does it end?" I ask John.

"Off the record?" he says, looking back over his shoulder towards the bathroom. Marie-Yves is still in there. The water is running through the pipes. John turns off the recording device. "To be honest, I don't know. Nobody knows except Bernard. I have a good idea though. Most likely I kill the guy and fuck the girl. That's how most movies work."

I press the record button and tap the microphone to verify that the red light triggers. "So, tell me about the girl," I say, sliding the recorder in front of him.

JOHN: She's a vampire. To be more phylogenically precise, a spider-whore, *arachnid latrodectus*. Phylogeny recapitulating ontogeny, art mimicing life.

STU: And the guy?

JOHN: Which guy?

STU: The one you are to kill.

JOHN: Pinocchio. The pimp. He is the leader of this cult of blood-sucking arthropods. He's more closely related to a mosquito than his victims, who for the most part become crawdads. Ontologically speaking. If mosquitoes could be made from wood.

STU: Given the historical connotations of his name, is it safe to assume his nose grows when he tells a lie?

JOHN: That's the crude assumption. The means by which he infects his prey is through his proboscis. Mind you, this is all a drug-induced fantasy in the mind of the protagonist. He goes to Paris to write a screenplay and gets writer's block. The bellboy scores him drugs and a prostitute and that's all he needs to dream up the story. He never even leaves his room.

STU: Are you talking about the actual screenwriter, Bernard? Or the screenwriter within the movie?

JOHN: My character. Troy. The protagonist in the movie.

STU: This all sounds familiar. Hasn't this story been done before?

JOHN: Which part. The guy going to Paris and hooking up with the prostitute and drugs?

STU: More specifically the way it is a movie about writing the movie he's within.

JOHN: But has anybody combined these two concepts? The growing film archive is like our collective genome. Every film is a splicing of two other successful films, where success is determined by the ability to 'survive' the box office. It's survival of the fittest. You're allowed two minutes to pitch a movie to a studio executive. There's no time for foreplay. There's only enough time to marry two stories he is already familiar with into one recombinant nutshell.

STU: Let's get back to the film at hand. Who plays Pinocchio?

JOHN: Big Bubba Dixon.

STU: The porn star?

JOHN: You know him?

STU: Of him. I've never seen his movies.

JOHN: Yah, well, the director Bernard knows him quite well, or did. They were ex-lovers. He still gives him roles in all of his films. As well as Ron Jeremy.

STU: What about the spider-whore? In real life.

JOHN: Julie Delpy.

STU: How was she to work with?

JOHN: [sips water]. What can I say? She's even more stunning in real life. And to think that I'm getting paid to have sex with her! I can't complain.

STU: Well. You won't *really* have sex with her.

JOHN: They don't believe in faking sex here. Did you ever see the opening scene of *Betty Blue*? There was no faking that.

STU: Any off-screen sparks?

JOHN: Not yet. But she still counts in my book.

STU: What's your latest tally?

JOHN: I've killed 57 men and fucked 8 women. And I myself have never died.

STU: Way to go. Keep up the hard work. What does Marie-Yves Curie think of all this?

JOHN: There's nothing to think. It's all scripted.

Marie-Y is still executing her toilet. At least she'd like us to think so. It's just John and me and the recording device in the kitchen.

A weird French cockroach scampers across the felt floor and into one of the drains. Neither of us acknowledges it. John wants to get off the topic of the movie and back to the subject of bald supermodel strippers, saying they are so unreal it's not sexual. He goes into in the evolutionary genetics of it, and our genetics for desiring them. I'm trailing off, mesmerized by the red light on the recording device, wondering what's taking Marie-Y so long.

"Well," John waves his hand in front of my eyes. "Do you?"

"Do I what?"

He turns the recorder around so it's facing me.

JOHN: Do you think my little platypussy is worth it?

(I don't answer but he goes on weighing the pros and cons like she is an investment opportunity. He doesn't "want to settle," but he has a "vested interest" in her. She has good teeth, but does she have the assets to counterbalance her lack of breasts, her soft orange underbelly and smoking habit, which could very well be genetic? He says there are other "special" things about her, but he doesn't specify.)

JOHN: In the end I'd rather die than settle for anything less.

Stu: Less than what?

This time it is John who doesn't answer. We leave the recorder running, but stop talking. I turn off the recorder but he turns it back on. When I ask why he gives his stock answer: "If it's not rolling, we don't exist." We sit there sipping our coffee until Marie-Y re-emerges from the bathroom wrapped in a white towel, still dripping, puddling all over the floor.

"How you can understand it here with all this light?" she asks.

"Stand," I say. Marie-Y squints at me suspiciously, like she is having a hard time seeing me despite all the light. "Stand is what we say when you can't tolerate something. You can't stand it."

"That is a funny thing to say."

"And *under*stand is to comprehend."

"And you suppose are a stand-*in*?"

"Don't even bother trying to understand," says John, "And why bother with the towel if you're gonna stand there dripping all over the place?"

"Is this what all the dreams are for?" I ask. "—I mean drains." Neither of them notices my slip.

"I don't like to rub on myself," says Marie-Y. "It is not health-wise to rub, you know. One should always let a body dry naturellement. En plus, this is my habitation."

"If it's your habitation then why do you need the towel at all?" asks John.

"Because it is your brother here. Or at less this is what it is you want me to believe." She eyes the recording device. "To who you are talking?"

"No one."

"Why do you have on the magnétophone?"

"I'm practicing my lines."

She grabs the recorder and turns it off. John lunges for her. She twists out of his grip and her towel falls off. She makes no attempt to hide her body. John wasn't lying about her breasts. They are nothing to write home about. And she is very white under the artifice lights, except for her orange belly with a scar-line running through it. Marie-Y rewinds a second and it makes a high pitch garbled hiss. She pushes play.

"*You know him?*" The recorder says. The same voice answers, "*of him. I've never seen his movies.*"

"Stop it!" says John, reaching for the recorder. Marie-Y fast-forwards and presses play again.

"*—to go. Keep up the hard work. What does Marie-Yves think of all this?*" Marie-Y is standing there, holding the magnétophone, still naked and dripping. "*There's nothing to think. It's all scripted.*" Marie-Y listens to the silence for a few beats and tries to fast-forward and press play again, but she must have inadvertently pressed the record button. It sounds like she listens to the silence we recorded for a few beats, then tosses the recording device down. Then she throws something else on the table in front of John, what sounds like the tail of a shrimp.

MARIE-Y: This is sucks. What does Oph think of this? Or Troy or Stu? I would like their opinion to know.
JOHN: It looks like the wing from a cockroach. You have roaches in your habitation, platypig.

(I try to interject, but the recorder doesn't pick up my apologetic denials. I feel responsible even though I'm not there.)

MARIE-Y: It's from an écrevisses. Obvious it is some prop you are using to get in the character. Admit it, you cheat. You use these things as, as crutches. You can't just be for one minute who you are.

JOHN: I'll be the first to admit I'm a method actor, but Stu's the one that brought this tail into our habitation. He probably brought it from back home in Georgia, as a joke.

MARIE-Y: I'm sick of hearing about this Stu. I'm sick of it all these lies and the, the role-plays. I want to just you be John.

JOHN: What about Oph?

MARIE-Y: D'accord, you can be Oph. But your brother he creeps me out. Around him a different person you become.

JOHN: Don't worry, pussypig. You're the only real thing for me.

[Sucking noise followed by the sound of a slab of raw meat slapping the table.]

MARIE-Y: It's not clean, Johnny! There is crumbs all over. [Sound of butter knife falling to the floor. Marie-Y sighing.] Not another Last Tango scene. It is before been done, thirty years ago. Please! No more butter. I just did my toilet! No dairy in my craw! It will get infecté. Je veux dire, Marlon Brando now is dead. Why you can't just be who you are?"

[Sound of recorder being shut off.]

Act II

Act II: Scene i
Hair of the Claw that Bit You

INT. Day. Hotel Room in Paris. Circa 2000.

Focus on:

Troy's unplugged computer in the foreground of a dark room. Unfocused door in background. Sound of knocks on the door. A pause, followed by the sound of keys scraping in the lock.

Zoom and focus on:

Back of door opening (unfocused, unplugged computer remains in foreground). The stereotypical French maid enters the room.

Pan (from maid's P.O.V.):

Around the room. The bed shows no sign of being slept in, except the top cover has been ripped off and thrown across the room. An unopened Trojan condom is on the bedside table. A chair is tipped over in front of her. She puts the chair upright. Then smells the pillow on the bed.

She goes into the bathroom. She feels then smells the towels. The soap has been taken out of the wrapper but appears unused.

Cut to:

Maid leaning over to plug in a cord.

Flash insert:

European male 2-prong plug inserting into European female 2-holed jack.

Back to scene:

As she leans over we glimpse her cleavage. The camera pans out to reveal a vacuum cleaner, the old fashioned kind with a cylindrical core sprouting a

56

ribbed tube capped with a phallic nozzle attachment.
The maid starts methodically vacuuming, sucking up
everything in her wake.

Flash on:

Tray of discarded crayfish shells and claws.

Cut to:

The maid takes the tray of crayfish carcasses and
places them outside the door. Returns to her
vacuuming, humming to herself.

Close up on:

Phallic vacuum nozzle going back and forth across the
same piece of brown shag carpeting. Over and over,
grinding harder. Individual carpet strings have the
texture of pubic hair.

Cut to:

Maid shuts off the vacuum and gets down on all fours,
inspecting the carpet. She sniffs at it,
scrutinizing.

Zoom in:

Closer on hair carpet, revealing grit, lint, fish
scales, milky stains and dried blood. Zoom in further
until macroscopic elements come into view—roots of
hair, skin flakes, mites, blood cells, ... all the
way down to DNA. What looks like a mosquito's
proboscis comes into the picture.

Cut to:

Handheld camera pans into the room, accompanied by
BUZZING SOUND. We angle around the unmade bed until
we get a voyeuristic view of the maid from behind,
her dress hiked up, a red garter belt exposed. Flash
of her black widow tattoo on her thigh. She picks up
something and rubs it between two fingers, sniffing,
then sits back on her heels. We continue to zoom in,
aiming for her neck. The buzzing intensifies.

Fade to Black.

Between Fish and Father

EXT. Day. Gaston Sewage Treatment Center, Savannah.
March 5, 1981.

I held the rusty barbed wire for him as he bellied under. John did the same for me from the other side. We snaked under, writhing forward in the red clay of the levee that held back the reservoir.

"Say it," John said, looking past me as I bellied under. He stomped his foot down right in my way.

"Cross my heart, hope to die, stick a needle in my eye."

John pulled his muddy foot out of my way. "Now hurry up. If we're caught in here we're dead."

Our mother would know after the fact. She always did. The red clay stains on our bellies were a dead give-away. All that mattered to us was now. We slid down the weedy embankment to the edge of the containment pond where we took off our shoes. Even though it was overcast, we each had four shadows from the artificial lights.

"This is it," said John, wading into the water. "This is where they are. You can tell by the oily trails they leave behind." He reached his hand under the rusty water and pulled out a crawdad that was bending its claws backwards to get at him. "You have to get them behind the claws." He grasped the crawdad's pincer. "Or you can grab the bull by the horns." He ripped the claw off. A torn white tendon flapped about where the claw was. He held the claw out to me like he himself was a crawdad.

"It's still alive on it's own accord," I said.

"Those are just reflexes. It's not technically alive." He dropped the crawdad back into the water and pinched me with the twitching claw.

"You're mean."

"It'll grow back. Happens to them all the time when they fight. You try it now."

"Why?"

"Just shut up and do it."

-3

My arm bent backwards where it hit the water. It was hard to judge the distance and the angle with a second elbow like the very crawdad I was after. The crawdad curled up his tail and spurted backwards, stirring up the settled mud and leaving a wake of silt.

"You got to be quicker," John said. "Try that one, she's got no claws. Battle wounds probably."

"How do you know it's a she?"

"You'll learn these things as you get older."

I let the ripples settle and looked down through the surface. The crawdad didn't have much color. She was more pallid than the surrounding clay. I brought my hand down above her then pinched her sides. The crayfish squirmed and her tail sputtered backwards, but she couldn't get anywhere. I pulled her out of the water and flung her up on the bank. "Something's wrong with this one. Her shell is all soft."

John examined the anemic crawdad on the red bank. He poked at her with his finger and flipped her over on her back.

"She's sick," I said.

"She's just molting." The crawdad squirmed and flailed. "They do that before they have babies. See." John uncurled her tail revealing a cluster of white globules. "There's the eggs. Told you it was a she."

"What are we doing here in the first place?" I asked, looking around back towards the fence. "Is this all worth it?"

"You have to go along with it or it's no fun," said John. "This one can be Aphrodite."

"But she's pregnant?"

"She'll be okay," he said, wading in. He grabbed two more. "This here is Helen. And this big one is Paris. Paris kidnaps Helen and—"

"Those aren't eggs on Aphrodite," I said. "Those are maggots." White worms were crawling from beneath, enveloping her. "This is seriously messed up."

"Whatever they are, they must need water to survive. They are freaking out now that they are out of their element." John lifted his foot and stomped on Aphrodite. She became embedded into the red clay, still writhing, pus oozing from her joints, worms swarming out from every crease in her armor. John stomped on her again and folded the clay over her. "Rice and crawdad pie."

"She's still alive."

"Those are just reflexes." He switched his attention back to the other crawdads. "Paris and Helen mourn the death of Aphrodite."

"But Aphrodite was a god. Gods can't die."

"Ours just did. Before she died, Paris picked her over Athena and Hera in a beauty agent. That's how he ended up with Helen. She was his consolation." John gathered up a few more crayfish and corraled them on the bank. "Helen was the fairest maiden in all of Achaea. All of the chieftain and Argive lords wanted to bone her, but they all swore a mutual oath of alliance and fidelity to whoever won her claw in holy matrimony. Eventually she became the wife of Menelaus."

"It's no wonder Paris made her the object of his desire!"

"Paris kidnapped Helen and set sail for Troy where, after several minor skirmishes, he built a fortified camp to settle in for an expected long siege." John and I sculpted a fort of mud and mulch, placing the crawdads into it. Then we gathered up a mamnewt army.

"Should we have a rehearsal first?"

"There is no rehearsing war. As the two armies draw towards one another, Paris—the instigator of all this—brashly steps forward and dares any of the mamnewt wizards to meet him in combat. The challenge is eagerly met by Menelaus, of all mamnewts." I placed a lethargic orange-bellied mamnewt in front of the crawdad we called Paris. "Paris is overcome by terror and runs away with his tail between his legs, hiding within the Trojan ranks."

"What a pussy," I said. "I bet he pees like a girl too."

"You're not alone in your thinking," said John. "Our father says the same thing whenever we get to this act. But Paris's brother Hector gives him a stern tongue-lashing and Paris agrees to the fight to save face. Of course Menelaus kicks his ass, but at the last minute Aphrodite intervenes, from the dead, and swoops Paris to safety."

"This is so contrived. And nothing is resolved."

"The repercussions unfold... "

Act II: Scene iii
Troy Flounders in the Alley

EXT. Night. Inside garbage can in alley, Paris. Circa 2000.

                                                        Flash on:

A BLACK CAT eating rotten seafood out of a garbage
can. The cat jumps out into a shadowy alley and
slinks past Troy, who lays passed out in a pile of
garbage with a needle sticking out of his arm. The
cat pauses and sniffs at Troy. Then continues down
the alley.

                                                        Cut to:

Troy wakes up and takes in his surroundings. Examines
his arms.

                                                        Flash on:

Pincers of a crayfish clawing at a dead fish, and
missing.

                                                        Cut to:

Troy floundering. He tries to grasp the dead fish,
but it appears he has lost all hand-eye coordination.
Troy moans in distress and attempts to crawl.

(Evidence of) the Roles We Wear

Next thing I know John is telling me: "don't just stand there." I'm not sure how I got here to begin with. I never am. "Make yourself useful," he says, pointing to the kitchen table where the recording device had picked up the sounds of their sexual act. "Help clean up this mess."

There are dishes and crumbs all over. Even the piece of crayfish tail that started all this. It doesn't feel like my responsibility, since technically I wasn't even here, but I grab some dishes off the table and hand them to John. "So what exactly does Marie-Yves do on the film?"

"Continuity," he says, throwing a wet rag at me. "She makes sure everything jives—that things flow smoothly from one scene to the next. See that table? If it's dirty like that in one shot, than it has to be the same configuration of dirty in the next. Unless you show someone cleaning it. My platypig would take a Polaroid of it so they could recreate the act."

As I'm wiping down the table under the stark artificial light, I see the smeared impressions of their sexual act that I had only heard previously. I wipe away the moist trails and am left with a handful of crumbs and the shrimp-tail. "Garbage?" I ask. John lets me get past him under the sink. I dump the crumbs and shrimp-tail on top of a used condom. The evidence is mounting. Unless the evidence was planted to deceive.

"It's an important job," says John. "And my platypussy does it well. Without her, our disbelief might not be suspended. She also doubles as the script coach. That's how I met her. She was running me through my lines and I didn't hear a word she was saying I was so engrossed in her lips and the way they were saying things. She's the only one on the movie that even speaks English. Except Bernard, but he's a prick. He thinks just 'cause we're in France we should be speaking French."

"Then why'd he write the movie in English?"

"Exactly," John says, glancing at his watch. "Shit, we gotta get rolling." He downs his coffee. "Platypig! Allez!"

"I coming," she yells from the bedroom.

John lifts the table and latches it to the wall.

"What do I need?" I ask.

"Nothing," he says. "Just your self. All you have to do is stand where you're told to stand. They might ask you to walk around or do some of the basic actions Troy does—while they set up the tracking and the lights. And ninety percent of the time you are standing in, you will be waiting around to stand in. Don't get your hopes high—it's not a glamorous job. Come on pigpussy! Let's roll!"

"Are you going like that?"

John is still wearing his Popeye pajamas, tops and bottoms. "No point in getting dressed. They'll do me up as Troy or Crawdaddy-O." He grabs a leather jacket out of the closet and throws it on over his pajamas. "Like you're one to talk," he says, taking my shirt between his thumb and forefinger.

I brush off my collared yellow polo shirt with a Razorback logo on it then tuck it into my khakis. "Everything I wear I got from you. These are your hand-me-downs."

"I wouldn't be caught dead wearing those threads—even ten years ago. Don't be telling anyone on the set you got those from me. We'll have to get you some new threads on your day off. You can't be walking around Paris like that. Come on platypussy! If we don't roll, nothing happens. Everyone's waiting for us." Marie-Y emerges in leather pants and a brown furry shirt. "You got the keys?" asks John.

She pats herself down, then reaches under her fur shirt and pulls some keys out, rattling them in her hand, snapping me out of it. Marie-Y almost shuts the door on me before I manage to slip through down the hall to push the button for the elevator.

"That thing never comes," says John, brushing past me. I follow them as they wind down the stairs around the exposed cast-iron elevator shaft. We emerge out the front gate and onto the street. I step in something. I lift my shoe and it's gobbed with shit. "Welcome to France," says John. "Where they don't believe in cleaning up after their dogs."

I'm left looking at my sole's impression in the smeared dog shit. As John and Marie-Yves argue about where the vehicle is parked, I scrape my shoe on the edge of the curb. Zooming in, down to ground level for closer inspection, I see hair, feathers and shellfish remains in the shit. There's a funny smell coming from a nearby drain that induces me to remember my dream from the night before.

The Adjoining Room at the Calico Hotel

INT. Night. Dream Sequence.
September 23, 2005. 1:51 a.m.

Marie-Yves and I went to "get a room." When we arrived at the hotel the lobby was full of cats—orange tabbies that all appeared to be related. One in particular, with tear-duct markings like a cheetah, rode with us in the elevator. It had some sort of nerve disorder that rewired its intentions. If it tried to jump to the right, it jumped to the left. If it tried to jump up, it slunk to the ground. This cat had learned to make do by always thinking the opposite of what it wanted to do, so by not trying to get in the elevator with us, it ended up in the elevator. Initially I thought by the way the cat was rubbing against me that it truly wanted to ride up with us, until I realized it might be rubbing my leg against its will, and that in its heart it truly despised us.

I was embarrassed because I was the one that had suggested this hotel to Marie-Y, who by this time (judging by the ruby ring on her finger that evidently she had received from me) had become my fiancée. The cat tried to rub against her leg but fell in the opposite direction away from her.

"I'm sorry," I kept saying.

"Don't worry," she kept saying back, touching my elbow. "There's nothing for you can do." Then Marie-Y started rubbing against me with increasing intensity.

When we got to our floor, the hall was full of identical calicos. They all got out of our way as we approached like a sea of cat molecules parting. They bowed down on their front paws in perfect unison and avoided eye contact. The orange cat with the nerve disorder and tear-duct markings remained in the elevator as the doors closed behind us.

"Sorry if this is weird for you," I said.

"Not to worry. It puts me in the mood."

Our room key said 'habitation 16-28-13,' but all the doors had X's or Y's on them. The room at the end had a bank vault door with a combination lock.

"Ah-hah," I realized. "Maybe it's not the room number, but the combination." There was a funny smell coming from under the door, making me reluctant to even try it. One of the cats lifted its tail and sprayed on the door, effectively counteracting the smell.

"We're rich!" yelled Marie-Y. She hugged me and I accidentally kissed her on the lips thinking she was coming to kiss me, not realizing that the custom here was to kiss to either side on the cheek. Marie-Y kept kissing me back, on the lips, and then with an open mouth and I reciprocated. She tasted like she had eaten an orange, or some orange-flavored candy.

"Why?" I asked, after we had finished kissing.

"The Muséum National d'Histoire Naturelle pays 10,000 euros to anyone that encounters a male calico." When we looked down, the cat had mixed in with the others.

"They all look the same to me."

"Only one of them is a male, with XXY chromosome instead of XY."

"How will we be able to tell?"

"To lift their tails and verify."

When we walked toward the cats, they kept sweeping just out of our reach. Marie-Y got down on all fours, meowing like she was one of them—thinking the male might act differently toward her.

Savannah Woman Jumps From Casino Boat

TYBEE ISLAND, GA, April 3 — What started as a leisurely outing with her husband aboard the John-of-Ark turned into tragedy Friday evening for a Savannah woman. Mary Xavier White, 34, presumably drowned yesterday off Tybee Island. She was last seen wandering the deck of the ship in rough seas.

"I saw her open the gate in the stern and just go a walking right off," said Larry Butler, the deckhand, reputably the last person to see her alive. "She said something about wanting to swim with the dolphins. I didn't think she was actually serious."

She had reportedly been drinking and had lost a considerable sum of money at roulette. This, aggravated by a clinical history of disassociative hysteria, presumably led Mrs. White to jump from the boat. Pending further investigation, officials have not yet ruled whether the alleged death will be considered as suicide or accidental.

"This is not the first incident we've had with this woman," said Captain Clark Smith. "We've had problems with her in the past." According to Smith, she and her husband were regulars on the John-of-Ark. She had a problematic history of drinking and gambling binges aboard the boat. In one such incident last September, she was so disorderly she had to be detained by being handcuffed to the rail until they reached shore, whence she was turned over to the authorities.

The death has caused officials to reevaluate the legality of the gambling law in Georgia. A loophole in the current law makes an exception if you are three miles off the coast in international waters.

"I don't understand why anyone would want to pay fifty-five dollars just to get sick off over-priced alcohol, lose all their money at tables with crappy odds, and to top it off, get all seasick," said the investigating officer, Joseph Gallagher. "But nevertheless, I reckon those individuals should be left with that right to choose."

Due to unseasonably rough seas, the John-of-Ark was unable to turn around and look for Mrs. White without endangering the rest of the passengers and crew. The Coast Guard searched until Saturday evening when the search was called off. The police also combed Tybee's beaches but no bodies were found.

Mary X. White is survived by her husband Calvin White of Savannah, and their son John.

Rehearsal for a Shotgun Wedding

EXT. Rue D'Escole, Paris.
September 23, 2005. 7:44 a.m.

John says it smells like something died but I don't think it's quite that. There's also a strange clicking noise emanating from the drain. Something is eating away at something down there.

"My platypig doesn't even know her own car," John says. By this time Marie-Yves has splintered off in the search. Evidently you have to watch where you park here or the police will tow it. Or it will get stolen. John is distraught. He puts too much importance into the car, says it's more than a car—calls it his transcendental soul. He calls the car by its brand name— Nandi. This is what he is saying, but sometimes I wonder if I know who John is—whether he is not in my head.

Something sparkles in the drain. I reach through the drain grate to a hidden lip before it goes down further. It's moist with a filmy moss. John's voice is still echoing around down there. As I'm feeling around I'm wondering if any Parisians have ever reached around in here. The whole history of the drain flashes in a split second—the storms, the hosed-down fires and the blood washed from the streets. I find something hard and smooth. It's a ring. Looks to be real silver with a red stone. I recognize it from my dream. I show it to John. "Could be a ruby," I say. "Might be worth something."

He quickly dismisses it. "It's probably a fake."

"You can at least give it to Marie-Yves."

"You found it, you give it to her."

"It would feel funny coming from me."

"It might be a swell gesture coming from you. Just don't mention you found it in a gutter."

We continue to search for the car. All the streets look the same to me. There's no planning this type of chaos. Dwellings and streets have sprouted up like weeds. People hustle to and fro without even giving notice to us. Despite the lack of order, everything has established permanence. I follow John as he walks in a circle, ending up back in front of the habitation just in time for Marie-Y to pull up next to us in a flesh-colored Nandi.

"Shotgun!" says John, opening the passenger side. He slides the seat forward so I can squeeze in back.

"Who is it has a gun?" asks Marie-Y.

"It's a figure of speech," he says. "In America it means you want to sit in front."

"Who else might sit in front?"

"Stuart."

"Oh yes, of a course. Stuart. How I could forget. I didn't know if he here lived on public."

We get in and Marie-Y pulls the Nandi out into the alley. She turns to me like she is interviewing me, "tell me Stu, does everyone in America carry the gun?"

"Absolutely," I say. "Especially us rednecks from Georgia. We have nine-hundred-pound hogs to contend with. We also customarily lose our virginities with our sisters."

"That's the spirit!" says John. "I tell you platypig, once my little brother gets in character, he's good." John eyes me through the space between the seats, speaking to me through the corner of his mouth like a ventriloquist, "I'm going to see about getting you a part in this movie."

"You are scaring me Johnny," says Marie-Y. "This goes too far."

"I better not hear *Johnny* come out of your mouth on the set."

"You the one who is gives me all this names to remember," she counts on her fingers while she is driving, "Oph, Troy, John, Stu, Crawdaddy-O."

"There's one name to remember—Oph."

"What about this brother Stu?"

"You can forget about him for the time being," he says, then turns back to me. "If I get you a part and you speak, even just a few words, you'll get five hundred bucks. And automatic membership to the Screen Actors Guild. Then you'll be somebody."

Marie-Y weaves the car in and out of heavy traffic. If I can see her in the rear view mirror, then I must be in her way. I slide over to the side. Out the window I glimpse the Eiffel Tower in the distance. It looks just like it does in postcards. I pinch myself. We're flying through the streets of Paris in a Nandi.

"You know what they call a virgin in Georgia?" I ask Marie-Y. She doesn't answer. "A girl that can run faster than her brothers." Marie-Y doesn't laugh. Now I can see her in her side mirror. She doesn't know it. Despite the laws of physics, I can see her but she can't see me. There are French words embossed on her face that I assume mean something like "objects in mirror are not as close as they appear."

"This is sucks," says Marie-Y, lighting a cigarette. "This fucking traffic." She exhales and her jaw pulses in the side mirror. She honks the horn and yells in French at other drivers. From this angle, Marie-Y looks like pictures I've seen of our mother when she was younger. Our Mother the Fish, as we used to call her. Oph is yelling at Marie-Y to put out her cigarette and watch her driving. He rolls down the window. A moped almost takes his arm off. We start moving again. All the air comes back to me, but I don't care. I don't even care about the cigarettes or Marie-Y's maniacal driving or the fact that I have no idea where we are and where we're going. I'm in Marie-Y's hands. Despite the traffic, we're getting there. We hit every green light. Every lane change gets us in a faster lane. We squeeze through openings I never thought existed. For the first time, I'm glad to be here in Paris.

Oph rolls up his window and the car fills back up with just us, waking me up. Marie-Y cringes her nose in the side mirror. "What is this smell?"

"That would be Stu," says Oph.

"Sorry," I say. "I stepped in it."

"You blame everything on this Stu," says Marie-Y. "And keep all the good stuff for yourself."

"That's the idea," says Oph. "Stu is here to exercise Oph's demons"

The smell reminds me about the ring. "Look what Oph had me bring you from Georgia," I say, wedging my hand between the seats to show her.

"This was all Stu's idea," says Oph.

She puts her finger out and without thinking I slide the ring on. She accepts it, like she's been expecting it. "Thank you, Stu," she says.

"The part he's not telling you is that he found it in the gutter." Marie-Y blows a lungful of smoke in his face. "It's true," he says.

"So," says Marie-Y. "Why do you have to go in and ruin it? I was getting to use this idea of Stu."

"Don't get too used to him. He's only here temporarily."

What Remains in the Lint Trap

INT. Day. Savannah, Georgia.
March 5, 1981.

John and I came home late, red clay staining our clothes. The mulchy mud from the sewage pond caked on our shoes. Our mother had a fit before we even stepped through the front door. "Stop right there, mister. Leave your shoes and clothes on the porch."

John and I stripped down to our underwear. "We caught a ten-inch salamander," I said. "In our crawdad trap."

Our mother ignored me. "Hand me your soiled garments," she said, taking the dirty clothes from our hands. "And go wash up. Lord knows what you've gotten into. Then go set down to eat. Your meatloaf's getting cold—the meatloaf I've been cooking all day just for you."

Before she put our things in the washer, she went through the pockets. She pulled a quarter out of my pants.

"Hey!" I said, "That's mine!"

She stuffed my pants in and started the cycle, acting like she didn't hear me. Then she pulled the lint trap from the slot in the dryer and swiped it. "Go wash your hands now."

"That's his quarter!" John said.

"Finders keepers, losers weepers." She wadded the lint into a ball. "You shouldn't neglect these things. This is the only way you'll learn."

I ran to our mother. She hid the coin behind her back. I grabbed her around the waist, my head buried into her lap. She smelled of laundry lint and meat loaf. I grabbed at her hard but she was oblivious to me.

"Give it to him!" John said. "It's his."

"Quit looking to your imaginary friends for help."

"He's my brother. Your son."

"You're eight now. You need to learn these lessons for yourself." I finally got a hold of her fist. Her fingers surrendered to me but all I

71

got was a ball of lint. The other hand slipped into her pocket. I heard the coin mixing in with hers. I grabbed at her but she was slippery as a fish.

John jumped in to help. Seeing him in his white underwear made me realize that I too was only wearing underwear. I felt encouraged and empowered when there were two of us, both down to our underwear. John pulled our mother's fisted hands behind her back while I rifled deep down into her pockets, then twisted her inside out. The coins scattered all over the linoleum. We pounced on them like the contents of a broken piñata. At least I did. She managed to grab John by his arm and slap him. "You need help young man." She didn't scold me even though I wished she would instead of him. It was my quarter that started all this.

"You slap like a fish," John sang to her. "And you smell like one too."

"That's some way to speak to your mother! I slave for you all day and this is what I get?!" Our mother left the room in hysterics, leaving a trail of wetness in her wake.

"Look who's the one who trailed a mess into our home now," said John, accepting the coins I handed to him off the floor. "Not us. Our Mother the Fish."

The Temporary Occupation of Hazard

EXT. Boulevard Gambetta, Paris.
September 23, 2005, 7:52 a.m.

We're accelerating through the now wet streets of Paris in a flesh-colored Nandi. The world revolves around us. Marie-Yes caves in to Oph's bitching and turns the windshield wipers on. "It is wipe the bugs around and makes it badder," she says. "For yourself you'll come to see." Time is folding in, but expanding at the same time, with the wipe of each blade. I fall in and out of sleep. We can't see the outside of the car from the inside, especially through a smearing windshield, but Oph reminds us every two minutes of the flesh-colored Nandi we are traveling in. He doesn't necessarily like the color itself, just the self-conscious idea of it. He also believes that a Nandi is a discrete unit of travel, akin to the euro being a unit of currency. Everyone on the street might have a Nandi, but according to Oph, ours is the only one that is flesh-colored. Our way is guided by expanding neon-green crosses. I ask if they are churches but Marie-Y says they are "drug places." There's one on every block, every one with the same pulsing neon plus sign, expanding and contracting at the same rate as my own breathing. I am starting to feel sick from Marie-Y's cigarettes and crazy driving but I'm beyond caring. She is so busy yelling at pedestrians that we can't hold a conversation.

Oph is rambling on another wavelength—everything he says starts with, "they don't believe in…" This is his way of filling me in. They don't believe in traffic lights here. They don't believe in underwear. They don't believe in the bottomless cup of coffee. They don't believe in personal space or non-smoking sections. They don't believe in deodorant. "For that matter," says Oph, "they don't believe in obeying any laws. Mind you, this is Paris. The beliefs of Studio la Suture are an even more absurd subset." Oph rolls down the window and sticks his head out.

Marie-Y says because his "glass" is down, the smoke is blowing his way. Oph informs her it's called a "window." She asks what the difference is between glass and window and Oph doesn't know, except that when a window breaks it becomes glass and that regardless, her cigarettes make us sick. But if Marie-Y doesn't smoke she'll get in "an incident," as she calls it. "Accident," Oph says. This is followed by a moment of euphoric silence at high speed, winding through jaded wet streets with no apparent design. What I see flashing by is a permanent backdrop to those living here. Everything in the outside world is falling asleep in me as we accelerate. It feels good to be out of control with Marie-Y at the wheel. An ambulance flies by, the siren in no way resembling the ones back home. The streets are not planned civilly, but are warped by years of collective and subconscious genealogy. What single mind could've staged all this? These streets that were made for pedestrians and equestrians are now flooded with cars and busses and glazed in the green light from the pulsing crosses. These streets that we were now driving, that are lulling me to sleep until Marie-Y honks and almost hits a man with a fluorescent vest standing in the road with a rod.

"Hey," I say, "That's me!" The surveyor looks up from his theodolite and shakes his fist at us. We hear Doppler-shifted shouts as we fly by. "That's what I do back home."

"You're the asshole that blocks traffic?" Oph asks.

I explain to them what exactly the survey crew is doing and how necessary it is. Both Oph and Marie-Y could care less. They just want to get to the safety of the studio. Evidently my monologue had shifted to explaining the finer difference between window and glass, in physical terms, because Marie-Y thanked me and asked Oph why he can't be like me. "How I am to learn except for you to tell me with words what is bad or good?"

"You know what a waste of time it would be if I corrected every grammatical mistake you made?"

"For less I try to speak your language," she says. "You are in my country and not you do try even to speak mine language."

"That's because your kind are so rude about it. If it wasn't for us, you'd still be speaking German. And as for you," Oph turns around and hits me side the head. "What did I say about this upstaging shit? Planting these ideas in her head. You better not do that on the set. Oph's got a reputation to keep."

"I'm the one living in your shoes," I say. "I've worn your hand-me-downs. I've lived in your shadow. And now I'm going to be your stand-in. It's only fitting."

"At least you know your place," he says, nodding, gazing forward out the windshield. "I'm telling you, it's only temporary—if you cooperate I can get you your own speaking role. For now, just listen to Oph and keep your trap shut on the set. And remember," he turns to me, fingering the budding horn on his forehead, whispering, "this is not here. Do not bring it up." Rows of copper-roofed five-story buildings fold away from us as we cross a river. "This is the Seine," Oph says. "We have a location shot on this bridge. I get thrown off and miraculously recover and get washed ashore near the Notre Dame."

"Notice the way in which goes the river," says Marie-Y. "This is sucks. The river it goes away from Notre Dame."

"Leave it to continuity to rain on our parade," says Oph. "That's the magic of movies. We can make it look like it's flowing the other way."

"Anybody that has been here to Paris knows the truth."

"Everyone in the world knows which way the Mississippi flows, but everyone bought into Tom Sawyer. I bet Samuel Clemens was kicking himself that the river didn't flow north — away from slavery and towards freedom."

"I think was it Mark Twain who wrote Tom Sawyer?"

"Same difference."

We cross the bridge over the river. "Are we almost there yet?" I ask.

"We're always there," says Oph.

Need a Boat Slough

EXT. Dawn. Gaston Slough, Savannah, GA
June 23, 2004.

When we revisited a job site, after a night's sleep, I often didn't recognize it. Even if it was a day's sleep, napping like we did, for lunch, under the canopy of trees until we couldn't stand the ants crawling on us, drinking our sugary sweat. We revisited sites for various purposes—to finish what we started, to tie in a neighboring site or to reoccupy a site whose originally staked boundaries were beyond recognition. And then there was the "grudge fuck," as our father called it, taming a site that on the first visit chewed you up and spit you out.

We first surveyed this particular grudge fuck[6] in a different state of mind. We hacked swaths through the bush, we set the stakes, we tied the flagging, we paced off steps, we shot angles, we balanced the rod and we sat on a GPS spot for hours to lock it down—to tie everything in. But it was on a different day at a different time. The tide was high and now it was low, it was winter and now it was summer, it was dry and now the air was supersaturated. The flagging had faded. The kudzu bushes and vines had grown over, covering the stakes we initially set. My own handwriting used to write the coordinates on the flagging was undecipherable. The barbed-wire fence was still there, but what sections remained were rusted through and covered with vines, becoming part of the landscape. We stopped to piss on it. We leaned on our bush-axes and drank cola, only to piss and sweat it out minutes later. We couldn't contain our own leaking. The boundaries were set, but the shoreline of the pond had changed. It was no longer the rectangular reservoir it once was and the sewage processing machinery was smothered in foliage—rusted into the red soil to become a useless ore body for future generations to call a "ruin."

All was in vain. Our attempts to tag space, to define the limits. Our father thought otherwise—he considered surveying to be some

---

[6] The Gaston Slough Sewage Treatment Center

sort of validation of who we were. But when mapped out on paper the landscape never came into focus for me. The delineation between land and water was in constant flux. What was once a cape was now erased off the map. The brackish water stagnated into levels in between water and land.[7,8] This particular site was officially *Gaston Slough*, but John and I already knew what it was.

On any given day, the tidewater could back up into the rivers and swamps like a toilet overflowing. The plots of land bled into one another. We had to have an experience in a plot to give it a frame of reference—the plot where the water moccasin bit me, where our father was passing a kidney stone, where somebody had dumped the dead bloated dog, where we scared the nudists taking pictures, where the magnolia tree was struck by lightning. It's given name on the map rarely stuck. Something had to happen there to mean something. Our father referred to Gaston Slough as the site that was so boggy we needed a boat. Eventually he shortened it to *Need a Boat* and this is how he labeled it on the map.

On most days we carried on for lack of anything better to do with our time. And because we were paid. To make the days go by faster, I acted like somebody else I longed to be—an explorer or a soldier or a hunter. I acted out stories in the landscape to keep my mind occupied. I dreamt of what I would do with the money or where I could go. If I had enough, I could redefine myself somewhere else. Hollywood even.

When our father and I got the assignment to reoccupy the Gaston containment reservoir, I felt violated. I didn't recognize the place on paper—it had been reduced to an orderly rectangle of land with a fence and a square pond. There was no life pictured in it. Our father didn't know the significance of this place where John and I used to go, before we became men.

When our father and I got to a site, we only talked on walkie-talkies. And we never "walked," it was always pacing, counting off, for a purpose. We were men with work to do. We'd break for lunch and eat

---

[7] Bog, swamp, baygall, marsh, mire, bayou, fen, muskeg, morass, estuary, culvert, lowland, recess, puxy, quag, quagmire, slough, sump, jheel, glade, etc.

[8] Different words for the same thing: ambiguous fertility.

sandwiches from zip-loc bags that mother packed us. We'd drink cola from plastic containers that we stuck in the freezer the night before.

When I told our father I'd been to this place before, he reached into his vest for his weathered pocket bible. He pointed to a dog-eared page as proof and said we'd all been here and all of this was here before us and it would all be here when we left. Then he read some scriptures. The first time I came to Gaston Slough as a real man I found a OUI magazine. I didn't tell my father and tucked it into my pants, bringing it out at lunch to peruse in the shade of a tree. OUI was special because it showed the pink parts that Playboy and Penthouse didn't. The juicy morsels. The problem was all the pages were half-bleached and worn, saturated in muck. They disintegrated right before my eyes as I flipped the sodden pages searching for something pink and wet and real.

When we reoccupied the site, the iron hubs or G-monuments that once designated an exact location in space-time were now engulfed in the quagmire. What was once set in solid ground was now wallowing in salty mud. Our attempts to apply order to the land had been sabotaged by the earth itself. Entropy had encroached. The land sunk as we walked on it. I kicked a cola bottle John and I had left behind when we were kids. The bottle, in the smitten image of our mother as our father used to say, was still there, exposed, for someone else to find. Nearby, was a flannel shirt,[9] waterlogged like animal fur, decaying in the stagnant pond. The Spanish moss drooped and drooled like candle wax dripping from the oak and sweet gum canopy that hung over our heads. We were in the bushy mouth of something bigger than we'd ever understand.

When I closed my eyes after a day's work, I would see the site we had surveyed that day, the bush-axe whacking, over and over, in search of the G-monument. Now, when I close my eyes on the set of this film, the memory of this is all I see. The water is rising right before my eyes.

---

[9] The initial survey before the reoccupation was on a cold brisk morning.

Defining the Boundaries

INT. Night. White's Residence, Savannah, GA
January 5, 2006.

slough[1] (sluf) *n.*

1. An outer layer or covering that an animal casts or molts.

2. A mass of dead tissue surrounded by lining tissue: shell husk appeal.

3. An inhabit that has been abandoned.

—slough[1] v.

4. To discord as undesirable (to the senses).

5. The shedding of the uterine lining in the tailings (of, say, a menstrual cycle).

slough[2] (slou, slow) *n.*

6. A stagnant swamp, briny marsh, bog or soft pond, especially part of a bayou slagheap, a backwater, or a miry place (from French *place:* street).

7. A depression or hollow brimming with deep mud or mire.

8. A state of deep despair or moral degradation.

Cape (kâp) *n.*

1. A sleeveless outer garment fastened at the throat and worn hanging over the shoulders (such as sworn in by Count Dracula). E.g. *"Do you feel a cape?"*

2. Headland, neck, point, ness, bluff, naze, bill, tongue.

3. A point or head of lamb projecting into a body of water: e.g. *"Do you swear you've been to Cape Fear and nothing but the cape?"*

Jaundiced Egg White

Now I'm on the set. I haven't done anything my first day except wait around and record my actions. That's all anyone seems to do around here. I'm already having to hold my breath to keep from falling sleep.

After traversing Paris, we finally got to Studio la Suture, where we parked the flesh-colored Nandi in this contraption that John calls an "id shuffler"—a 40-story concrete block with no windows. We drove the Nandi into a slot at the base and the attendant gave us a receipt. Then he pulled some levers and the car disappeared into the guts of the building.[10]

When we finally got into the studio, John introduced me around to the cast and crew, painting me as some sort of renegade redneck cop that drove a red and white Gran Camino just like Starsky & Hutch. Not that anyone could understand what he was saying, but the few people who did speak English knew better, asking me what I "did for real." I told them the boring truth: I was a land surveyor that drove our father's truck.

After John left for makeup and wardrobe, the crew huddled around me, sniffing me and smoking, asking me what it was like to be "Egg's brother."

"Egg's?"

Marie-Yves clarified, "Oph sounds close to œuf in French, of which mean egg. So everybody here names him Œuf Blanc, of which means egg white."

"And that makes you Jaune," one of the English-speaking gaffers said.

"My brother is John," I said.

---

[10] When John first arrived in Paris, the studio gave him his own Nandi. It wasn't flesh-colored, but black. On his first day, he parked it in the id shuffler and lost his receipt. They couldn't retrieve his Nandi without the receipt, so to this day his Nandi remains parked in the Studio la Suture id shuffler.

"*Jaune,*[11]" clarified Marie-Y, "it means 'yellow' in French, you know, the yellow middle of the egg."

"Yolk?"

"Yes," said Marie-Y. "You are Jaune d' Œuf, Egg Yolk. And Oph is Œuf Blanc, Egg White. Though your apparition is more pink less yellow." They all get a laugh at my expense.

"That's lotion," I said, rubbing my arm. "Calamine."

"Every god sees under this light. Make-up has a will to smother this, Jaune."

"Jaune sounds too much like John."

"Who's John?" someone asked.

"There," said Marie-Y. "Nobody knows of John here. For us, you must be Jaune. Stu makes for a funny sound in French. And Oph is Œuf."

They made me repeat it back in French. Then they all shook my hand, calling me Jaune, and the women sniffed my armpits and rubbed against me, which took some getting used to. Even the director Bernard introduced himself and sniffed me. He seemed decent despite all the things I had been warned about.

And here I am, *Jaune*, as in Yolk, waiting. What Œuf, or Egg, says will be the beginning of a lot of standing. He suggested I write a book while I'm here so that's what I'm doing. Marie-Yves is busy giving and receiving orders in French through a walkie-talkie. The French call them "talkie-talkies." Everyone communicates with talkie-talkies even if they are in the same room. They even gave me one with the name "Jaune" inscribed on it. There's a bank of chargers where I need to return it every night. I'm no stranger to walkie-talkies. I've used them to talk to our father.

I overhear them say Œuf quite a few times on the talkie-talkies, so I assume they're setting up a scene with my brother Egg in it. All communication is through the talkie-talkie, even if the person is right next to you. When I express my reluctance to use the talkie-talkie, Marie-Y says that I have to, "for accounting." I tell her I can't understand anything because it's all in French. Evidently the talkie-talkies translate both English to French and French to English. In theory. My first talkie-talkie was defective, or needed to be reconfigured. When they gave me

---

[11] From *jaundice*: (i) A condition with yellowing of the skin or whites of the eyes, often caused by obstruction of the bile duct or liver disease. (ii) Disordered vision. (iii) Affect with envy, resentment, or jealousy.

a new one, it was true—everything was in English. And what I said to them got translated to French on the fly. "This is in Œuf's contract," Marie-Y whispers to me. "We must talk English so this it is what Bernard does is have it so the talkie-talkies talk English for us. That way Œuf, he cannot sue the studio."

Bernard is recapping the scenes we're filming today. Troy will kiss Celia the Spider-Whore. And since Julie Delpy is playing Celia, that means Œuf, my brother Egg, will be kissing Julie Delpy.

"Does that mean I get to kiss Julie Delpy?" I ask Marie-Y through the talkie-talkie. "Not that I would mind, but it would be weird to kiss her and then have Œuf kiss her. Even it is just pretend. Over."

"You desire, Yolk! If something, will kiss you replacement it for lashes the whore of spider," answered Marie-Y's garbled voice via the talkie-talkie. She pointed with her antenna at a French blonde that resembled Julie Delpy, but wasn't her. "Except very that you must make obtain in measurement to frame the projectile. You do not need to go through par with the actions. Done." To make matters more confusing, Marie-Y is standing close enough to me that I can hear her speaking into the talkie-talkie in French, a second or two ahead of the botched translation.

From what I can gather, before the kiss is the brawl. I get beat up by a bunch of soldiers, one of whom is Henry Rollins. Evidently he's a famous ex-punk-rocker that happened to be traveling through so Bernard gave him a cameo. Marie-Y said they might use me as an actual double for Troy, if I want, which is a step up from a stand-in. If so, they'll pay me a hazard fee of five hundred "stitches"[12] a day. The idea is that Egg will be in the scene, and right before he gets hit, they cut and "replace egg with yolk," as the talkie-talkie translates. They don't want to risk that my brother Egg gets hurt. So I, Yolk, will take the punches for him.

---

[12] The studio uses their own unit of currency, called a "point" (in French), which translates to "stitch" through the talkie-talkie.

DVI DIN DIN DIN DIN I   PEAS
DIN DIN DIN DIN IIa   PE
DIN DIN DIN IIb   SP
DIN DTN DIN IIIa   PE
DIN DIN IIIb

IN THIS VAULT ARE DEPOSITED THE REMAINS OF

LIVE BAIT

TEMPORAL (NOT A LIVE REHEARSAL)

SISTER OF THE SAID
WHO DIED JANUARY 29TH 1805, AGED 70 YEARS

WHO DIED MAY 8TH 1812
AGED 56 YEARS

ACT III

SCENE I   :   TROY BELLIES UP
SCENE II   :   THE MAKING OF THE MAN WHO WOULD NOT DIE
SCENE III :   THE YOLK SHOOTS UP FOR EGG SHOOT
SCENE IV   :   "I" DREAM OF MARIE-YVES' HAIR
SCENE V   :   "I" GET CAUGHT WITH MARIE-YVES' PANTS' DOWN
SCENE VI   :   RETROSPECT FROM THE CLAM BED
SCENE VII :   TROY BECOMES CRAWDADDY-Ô
SCENE VIII :   MAKING POISSON CRU

in vitro infected
hepatocytes

Act III: Scene i
Troy Bellies Up

INT. Dusk. Porkfish Belly Bar, Paris.
Circa 2000.

Troy walks down a dark alley. Sees a lit sign.

                                        Flash on:

Bare light bulb hanging over a flickering sign that
reads PORKFISH BELLY ABORTION CLINIC.
                                        Cut to:

Troy hesitating, then entering the Porkfish Belly. It
is dark. The only light comes from beneath the bar,
illuminating the BARTENDER, and the stage lights on a
band in the corner playing lounge versions of Velvet
Underground songs. Troy reluctantly steps up to the
bar. He is the only one there besides the bartender,
a man sitting by himself at a table and the band.

                    TROY
          Is this the Porkfish Belly?

                    BARTENDER
          It eez what it eez.

                    TROY
          At least you speak English. Where can I
          find Pinocchio?

                    BARTENDER
          Der eez no one by that name here.

                    TROY
          I was told I could find Pinocchio here.
          I need some bug juice.

The bartender wipes off the bar in front of Troy even
though it is already clean. But he does not speak.

                    TROY
          Is there a secret password or something?
             (uncrumples a slip of paper from
              his pocket and reads from it)

Am I the jackass looking for the salt
mines of Pleasure Island?

                    BARTENDER
Sorry I can't help you.

                    TROY
          (crumpling the piece of paper)
Then maybe you can tell me where I
could find a two-twenty to one-ten AC
converter.

                    BARTENDER
          (stops wiping, sizes up Troy)
How may Ampères?

                    TROY
               (not confidently)
Sixty?

                    BARTENDER
You can find Pinocchio over there.

Troy throws the bartender a tip and makes his way
towards PINOCCHIO.

                                        Insert:

Lethargic and melancholy musicians doing a loungey
version of *Sweet Jane*.

                                        Cut to:

Troy approaching Pinocchio, who is sitting with his
arms crossed in front of him, toothpick in mouth.

                    TROY
          You Pinocchio?

                    PINOCCHIO
Who's asking?

                    TROY
Somebody at Jim Morrison's grave told
me I could get some of the pure stuff
here. Bug juice, from the salt mines.

                    PINOCCHIO
          (diverting his attention from
               the band, sizing up Troy)
You want to be arthropodic?

                         TROY
         I *need* to be.

Pinocchio fishes around in his mouth with the
toothpick. Dislodges a piece of white meat, pulls it
out and inspects it, then eats it off the skewered
tip.

                       PINOCCHIO
         Put one hundred stitches on the table.
         The bartender will give you what you
         want. Ask for a White Russian and look
         under the napkin.

                         TROY
         I need a needle too.

                       PINOCCHIO
                        (sighs)
         Ask the doorman as you leave. And take
         it outside, we run a clean joint here.

Troy leaves a hundred stitches on the table.

                       PINOCCHIO
         Hey.

Troy hesitates.

                       PINOCCHIO
         You need a lady friend tonight? To keep
         the bedbugs from biting?

Pinocchio points with his lips at a series of six
boat objects[13] hanging from the wall.

                         TROY
         Are those ladies or boats? (beat)
         Regardless, I'm good. But can you tell
         me where I might find a power
         converter? For real.

                       PINOCCHIO
                 (taking a sip of his drink)
         Couldn't help you there, mate.

_____

[13] Each 42 inches tall, hung "stern" up, with 5 finger holes in the "bow" at Troy's
groin level.

Band doing a loungey version of *Heroin*.

Troy bellying back up to the bar.

                    TROY
          White Russian.

The bartender places a napkin in front of Troy and
sets out making his drink: a concoction of milk,
pigeon eggs, caviar, clam juice and vodka. He shakes
it up and sets the drink down on top of the napkin.
Troy takes a sip and sets it back down.

                              Close on:

Inside of Troy's mouth, black caviar wedged between
his teeth.

                    TROY
          What kind of White Russian is this?

                    BARTENDER
          (removes drink but leaves napkin)
          You see no—seventeen sugar hell-o's—
          pure square cane-fixing clam-baked colo
          bactaridio.

Troy reaches under the napkin and grabs a small
tinfoil-wrapped packet. He exits the bar, soliciting
a needle from the BOUNCER on his way out.

Act III: Scene ii
The Making of *The Man Who Could Not Die*

EXT. Day. Bonaventura Cemetery, Savannah.
April 7, 1985.

I pinch off eye-drops of food coloring into the jug until it is pink as the Calamine lotion I use on my chigres. "Give me that," says John, grabbing the red food coloring and the gallon of milk. He unscrews the cap and empties the whole bottle into the milk. Shakes it up until it's good and red and instructs me to pour it over myself. I don't want to stink like cheese is my excuse. John insists it's blood, not milk. That I have to *believe* this for it to work. Even if it's red and sticky, I know it's milk. I saw the carton with my own eyes. He insists I can't think like this or I will never be somebody. He sloshes some across my chest. Most of it splashes off and dollops in the sandy soil, taking its time to soak in. Even if you don't believe it, at least make it *look* real, John tells me. I am more preoccupied with my ruined shirt. Our mother will kill us, I say. John says he'll take the heat. That the shirt was originally his. It's mine now. I'm the one who has to live with it, I tell him. John insists it will wash off in cold water. But not to wash it off yet, not until it's "a wrap." He pours some straight over my head. It feels clammy. I wonder how this must look to someone from outer space. How would we explain this? There are no mirrors to see myself. John is superstitious about them. He tells me to trust him. That he's my brother. He grabs the video camera off a tombstone. He got it the week before for his eighth birthday. The muggy air hovers. We are stuck in suspension. Sweat drips down my face and mixes with the sticky milk-blood. I'm thirsty but all there is to drink is bloodied milk. The air is saturated with decay. The wind is blowing from the north, purging wafts from the paper mill in Garden City. The pulpy fumes are thick enough to be liquid.

John calls me *The Man Who Could Not Die*. He says I want to die but I have been condemned to live forever. I can't release myself from the shackles of life. This is the premise. Right now I have cut myself open and am begging for mercy at my family tomb. Hence the blood. Which tarnishes the real names on these tombstones. It will wash off with the next rain, says John. With a megaphone, he directs me to writhe on the grave. "Die for me!" he yells. "With passion. You're a suicidal failure. Good, now roll off the tombstone and start digging."

This is where I draw the line. There's real people down there. Even if John says they won't bite. It's not sacrilegious if you're not religious, he claims. But it's too much for me. I tell him I can't do it. Fine, he says, pushing the camera into my hand, still rolling. He grabs the jug of milk and bathes himself in blood. Smears it all over. Get this, he says. He takes a swig of the bloody milk and lets it dribble off his chin and down his chest. He gurgles up more. Half the time I look over the top of the camera, unable to believe my eyes. The way it's framed extracts it from reality. Everything is slower through the viewfinder, removed from our world. John becomes a sequence of snapshots. He slurs through the side of his mouth, spewing directions between his blood-gurgling. "Are we rolling? Make sure you get the river in the background. And some of these trees. And the hanging moss."

"You ruined it," I say. "By speaking."

"We'll dub sound later."

John vomits blood and I don't know if it's real or not so I keep filming. Spanish moss and vines hang down from the trees. Everything carries its own weight, pulling to the ground. John throws up again. This time there are gristly food chunks mixed with the fake blood. The smell makes me nauseous. I recognize our mother's meatloaf. The hot air is thick, the gravity oppressive. Bright light bleeds into the sides of the frame. My own breath is fogging up the viewfinder. The shadows are ill-defined. It doesn't matter that we are in the shade, the heat transpires from the ground where it has been festering. There's no escaping it. John rolls onto a tombstone, grabs his bloody shirt and rips it off, smearing blood all over the white marble. He is altogether a different person through the viewfinder. The Savannah River in the background is slow-moving and brackish brown. Muddy and wide.

"Are you getting this?" John asks between tortured looks of anguish.

"Don't worry," I say.

He stumbles across tombstones, falling and clawing at the ground. "Get the details," he says, "the dirt underneath my fingernails." I zoom in close. He staggers around like a zombie with his hands outstretched. He falls, clutches a marble cross, gains his strength to stand back up. Gropes his way to a large mausoleum that entombs a whole family. Oglethorpe is etched in gothic letters on the marble. He gasps and grabs his throat. Pounds on the door, screaming. Then his knees buckle and he crumbles to the floor in front of the door and goes into some sort of seizure. That's when I first notice the lady in a pressed black dress waddling her way towards us. There's our mother, and there's other kid's mothers. She is not ours. She is twice the circumference of our mother and her skin is a dark shade. Even though she is not our mother, her waddling swagger carries harmful momentum. "John," I say, letting the camera drop to my side.

"What are you doing?"

"Somebody's coming."

"She can be in the movie if she wants. Keep it rolling, if it's not rolling we don't mean shit."

I take off running towards the river where we left our bikes. Looking back, I see John talking to the black lady. She grabs him by his bloody hair and starts to drag him away. John squirms and spins his way out of it and starts running. At first I think he is running away from her, but she doesn't bother to come after him. It's way too hot for mortals. John doesn't slow down as he nears. I take off running again, still clutching the camera. My heart is pounding in my chest. It is getting harder and harder to breathe. My blood is thickening to syrup. John is gaining on me. When I get to the bank of the river, there is nowhere left to go. I turn around to reason with John. He comes at me full speed, lowering his head into my gut. We both go tumbling down the bank of the Savannah River. John comes up swinging. He lands one on my stomach, and another to my kidney as I buckle. He gets up and kicks me for good measure. The red milk makes it more violent than it really is. The hair on my neck bristles despite the heat.

90

"How could you leave me high and dry like that? Some brother you are."

"I knew you'd get away."

"She got a lock of my hair. Who knows what kind of voodoo she'll do on me now. Did you at least get it all up to that point?"

"I don't know," I say, looking down at my empty, bloodied hands. We were in direct sunlight now. The bloodied milk curdled on us. The camera was down near the water. The water of the Savannah River that connected to the Intracoastal Waterway that connected to the Atlantic Ocean where our mother was last seen. John fetches it and rewinds to where we left off.

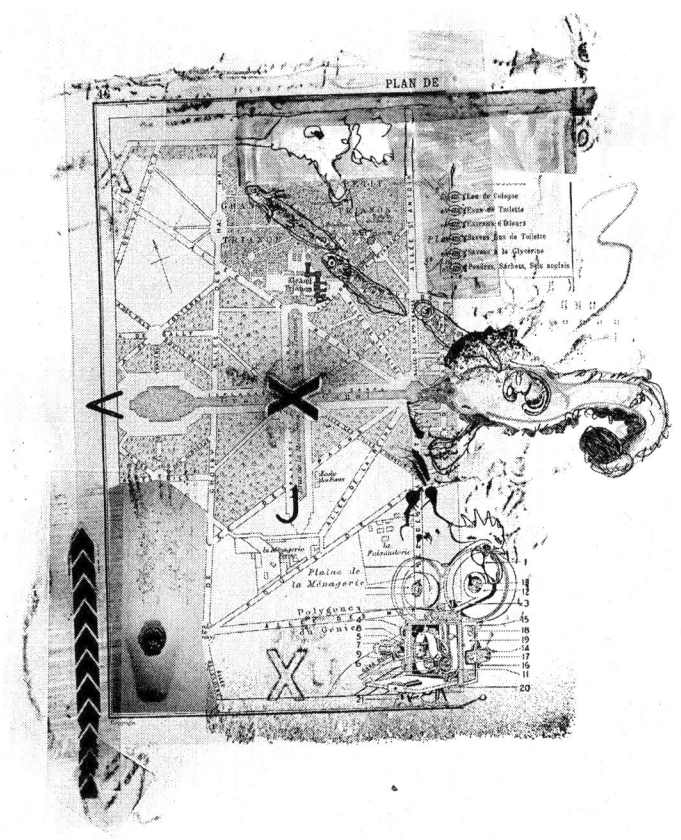

Act III: Scene iii
The *Yolk Shoots Up for Egg* Shoot

INT. Studio La Suture, Paris.
October 14, 2005. 3:04 p.m.

Egg[14] has a thing about needles—says he will pass out if he sticks one in his vein. Even at the sight of a needle penetrating skin. He can't even watch Marie-Yves self-administer her insulin. So I have to be the one. I don't mind—I'm being compensated five hundred stitches hazard pay for a few seconds of discomfort.

"If something, it will be of good health for you," Bernard says through the translating talkie-talkie. "Resembling an injection of vitamin. Done."

They've already filmed all the shots with Egg, where he prepares the narcotic bug juice, melts it in a spoon, gets the air bubbles out of the syringe—all the usual clichés. They've filmed up to where he ties off his arm and he's about to drive the needle home and that's where they cut. That was all shot on location. Now they're doing the insert shot of my arm shooting up here in the studio. Part of Marie-Y's job is to make sure the lighting from that location matches the lighting from this set. She also makes sure the special effects guy adds a scar to my right arm to match Egg's. The rawness from the recent molting of my arm—what I passed off as a bad sunburn—has toughened up back to normal.

Marie-Y and the makeup guy debate my arm in French, grabbing and twisting it like a sausage link. The makeup guy cakes on some gook that hardens into a welt, then powders my arm to match a Polaroid that Marie-Y took of Egg's arm.

"What did Egg tell you about his scar?" I ask Marie-Y directly. She is leaning over in front of me. I cop a look at the white skin beneath her shirt as it rises up to a pink nipple that is crinkled and chafed like a cockscomb. She is too busy matching my skin tone with a chart to notice me looking. Her fingers touch my arm. Her breath smells stale and diabetic.

"He says a fight with knife."

"The truth is we were climbing over a barbed-wire fence to get to this cesspool we used to play at. It was just a scratch but he let it get infected."

---

[14] Formerly known as Oph[†].
    [†] Formerly known as John.

"He said onto me that a group of Mexicans in Los Angels jumped him and cut him." She leans over and this time I can see the other nipple and even past it to her slightly distended belly.

All you'll see on film is the syringe and my arm, maybe a bit of the rubber hose at the edge of the screen. The director of photography's assistant is not on the set so Marie-Y fills in with the clapperboard. She is chewing gum, mouth open, reading off the clapper in English, "act seven, scene one. Insert—Troy shoots up." She doesn't clap it like they do in movies were they make movies within the movie, she just holds it there limp-wristed, long enough for the cameraman to film the scene information.

"Rolling!" says Bernard through the talkie-talkie.

Marie-Y pulls away and squats down, watching me. I cinch off the rubber hose and let my vein bulge. Then I stick the needle in and push the plunger. This is easy for me to do. I feel detached from my body. There are a few seconds of silence, except for the whirring of the camera. I'm not sure whether to pull the needle out. I start to drift off.

"Cut!" says Bernard. "Attend the slit." Marie-Y is in a stare at my right arm. She starts to chew her gum again.

"Sorry," I say through my talkie-talkie.

"For what?" asks Bernard.

"For falling asleep. Over."

"Here it is I believed you were acting. Done."

"Did you want me to pull it out?" I ask Bernard, releasing the strap. "On film? Over."

"No, that refine just," says Bernard via the talkie-talkie. "We will draw more for the checking, perhaps this time does it slower. With passion. Done." Bernard lights a cigarette then pats me on the back, his feet splayed like a duck. He holds the cigarette up and away from his body. "You know, Jaune, I like you. You are very cooperate," he says to me directly, blowing his first drag of smoke out. "Unlike your vile brother, Œuf."

I'm not quite sure how to respond to this. I want Bernard to like me, he's paying me to do all this. But not at Egg's expense.

The makeup crew tends to my arm. The set dresser takes the syringe from me and refills it with more vitamin solution. Marie-Y holds a wad of cotton to my arm, cigarette dangling from her lips.

Egg walks onto the set, half in costume—with a red velvet shirt, claws on his hands and antennae projecting from his head.

Bernard is still next to me, with his hand resting on my shoulder. I lean forward, trying to get his arm to drop clear of me, but it remains there. Bernard sees Egg, snorts, and walks away.

93

"Isn't that makeup's job?" Egg asks. Egg and Marie-Y don't usually speak on the set. He doesn't want the crew to suspect anything. "You're continuity," he adds, waving his claws around in an exaggerated manner to clear Marie-Y's smoke from his airspace.

Marie-Y continues applying pressure to my arm with the cotton ball. She releases it and takes a drag of her cigarette. There is no blood, just a barely noticeable puncture. "This is continuity," she says. "We can have not there be blood to notice."

"How did it go?" Egg asks me.

"Quick and painless."

"Thanks for shooting up for me. I don't know how you do it—how you ended up so normal and me such a squeamish freak. I can stand scrapes and bruises and surface wounds, but anything that gets under the skin… I can't even cope with the idea of it."

"Of agreement!" yells Bernard through his talkie-talkie, motioning for everyone to clear the set. The set dresser hands me the loaded needle and the director of photography passes his cigarette to his assistant while he gets behind the camera. Marie-Y stands in front of me with the clapperboard. I rest my arm on my knee, my hand outstretched, palm up.

"Oph can't watch this," says Egg, melodramatically. "Oph gets queasy just watching someone putting a needle in their vein."

"Silence!" Bernard yells. "Close your mouth, Egg!"

"What does it matter?" Egg says back directly. "You're going to dub Troy's voice over anyway. And my name is Oph, not Egg. Program that into your talkie-talkie."

"Do you direct me on how to direct?" Bernard asks. "You do not even have the just need for existing in this moment."   ·

"Oph doesn't want to be here right now," says Oph walking off the set, but not before turning to me. "Thanks again, bro, for taking up the slack."

"We shall roll!" announces Bernard.

Marie-Yves does the clapper again and I tie off my arm. The cameraman focuses in. I stick the needle in and squeeze the plunger. I feel the enriched liquid seep into my vein. I drift off.

"Cut!" says Bernard. "That's a good catch. Attend the slit."

Act III: Scene iv
"I" Spell Marie-Yves's Hair

INT. Day. Dream Sequence.
October 25, 2005. 2:13 p.m.

I acquired a lock of Marie-Yves's hair from the drain in her boat tub. It was long and shiny and the color of blood. Evidently the lock of hair had "specie" power. Waving it around through the air, I could feel the magnetic torque the strands were generating. When I turned off the lights, a mini-aurora became visible. When I stopped waving it, the lock of hair was actually a movie clapperboard made of black velvet. It was full of cryptic hand-written information about scenes from the movie that revealed itself under a "specie" black light. Instead of black and white diagonal stripes, the scissored clapper part had gene sequences on it—unique barcodes that contained all you needed to know to make the movie. Reading the instructions off the clapperboard I learned that I had one spell to cast.

I cut a lock of my own hair and "spelled" it together. I didn't want to question the instructions for fear it wouldn't work. My hair turned into these miniature 1-stitch bills, paper coins actually, that fell to the ground like leaves. When I stooped to examine the "stitch coins," they were glowing scales. I could tell by the underlying carpet the glowing scales were illuminating that I was back home in Savannah. Oph was there too. I hid Marie-Y's lock of hair in my pocket for fear he'd recognize it. Everywhere I stepped, these phosphorescent scales appeared. But it only worked with me. I could hear Oph moving around the dark room, talking to me, but couldn't see his footsteps. He was saying it must have been something I ate, radioactive fish probably, and that I should see a doctor.

I'd had enough of being in the dark. I tried to turn on the lights but they didn't work. I went into the dining room and tried the dimmer switch. The lights dimmed on to reveal a yellow chick whose chirping sounded like a Geiger counter. The chick's eyes were where the glowing scales had been. All the glowing scales were in fact chick eyes whose bodies appeared if I looked directly at them, but were otherwise invisible in my periphery. Armed with this knowledge, I dimmed the lights off and asked Oph to guess what the glowing dots were.

"What else would we be looking for on Easter morning?"

This changed everything. I felt a hand digging around in my pocket. I grabbed the hand and tried to pull on it, but it was like pulling on my own arm that was doing the pulling to begin with. "What are you doing?" I asked.

"I know you have an Easter egg in there," Oph said. "The Golden One."

"Is that what this is?" I asked. "An Easter Egg hunt?"

I took Marie-Y's lock of hair, which indeed had become a patterned egg, and threw it into the kitchen. Oph saw it flash by and went to fetch it. "Get a load of this," he said, turning on the light. "This is like the funniest thing ever." He started laughing hysterically. "This is where my platypus comes from."

I was afraid to look, but I had to see what was so funny. The chick was in there but it had grown into a white rooster with an oversized cockscomb. There was also a white rabbit that was trying to fuck the rooster, which confused the rooster more than anything. Our laughter confused him even more. His cockscomb was so large he could barely keep his head up. Our voices were scrambled and magnified over a loud speaker to sound like hens squawking. This made us laugh harder, which made the squawking louder and more frantic in a feedback loop with no threshold in sight.

Act III: Scene v
"I" Get Caught With Marie-Yves's Pants Down

INT. Day. Dream Sequence.
October 26, 2005. 1:25 p.m.

I woke up in bed with Marie-Yves on an island in French Polynesia. I'd never been there before but knew where I was. I was staring up at the palm frond ceiling thinking how good I had it. Marie-Y was sleeping next to me. Evidently we were part of a research team that was sent to Tahiti to determine why Pacific lobsters had no claws.

Then I felt something slithering beneath the sheets. I jumped up, naked from the waist down, throwing the sheet back. A black and white scorpion snapped its claws and flung its tail in my direction. Marie-Y's foot was swollen and blue. I panicked, wondering what to do: If I tried to get help, people would know we were sleeping together. The only thing going through my head was: This was how we'd be discovered. This would be what our relationship was founded on. I couldn't think straight until I put some pants on. But first I felt obligated to check Marie-Y's neck for a pulse. She woke up and asked what I was doing.

"I'm seeing if you're alive!" I said.

"Well?" she said.

"You're probably in shock. You were stung by a scorpion." I pointed to her foot.

"It is all the time been this way," she said.

"There was a scorpion in bed with us. It was right here."

"Probably you were dreaming. It means something."

Then I heard a buzzing sound above my head and felt a burning sensation on my scalp. "It's in my hair!" I leaned over so Marie-Y could check. She sighed and started sifting through my follicles. "Do you see anything?"

"Nothing but for these tiny red bugs," she said, picking one out and eating it.

"Those are chigres," I said. "They are not for eating!"

"It is nature."

"We don't have the proper enzymes to digest them."

"Pass right through me they will?"

"I guess."

"Then no harm in it."

The buzzing sound was getting louder and the itching more intense. I looked up at the ceiling and the palm fronds were teeming with red chigres. I jumped up and ran out of the hut screaming. Bernard and the film crew were all there outside our door, though they were really research scientists doing a documentary on Pacific lobsters. The lights and camera were pointed at our door. I emerged, exposed from the waist down, screaming and scratching myself all over. It was silent except for me and the whirring of the film in the camera. The past was catching up to the present.

"Is this all in the script?" I ask.

Bernard throws his hands in the air. Sheets of the screenplay scatter in the wind.[15] "Guillotine," he says, slicing his finger across his throat.

"You were good until then," said the cameraman, clapping.

"Were these chigres for real?" I ask.

Bernard answers in the negative, "they are in reality baby lobsters." This is followed by a realization that I am naked and that Marie-Yves is in my bed in the hut.

Bernard gathers the sheets of paper from the ground. "Of accordance, let's try this again. Remember Jaune, suck first the poison from her womb and then you get Marie-Yves to bite the head off the scorpion." He points to the script. "Just like it says."

"Wound." I say.

"What?"

"Suck poison from her *wound*. Not womb."

"How?"

---

[15] Generated by an industrial fan.

"Never mind," I say, thankful that none of it was real. When I go back into the hut, Oph is in bed with Marie-Yves. He looks just like me but it is in theory my brother.

"Action!" yells Bernard through a translating megaphone. I realize "I" am just a stand-in, so I hide myself in the closet. Through the slats in the closet I watch as Oph wakes up, discovers the scorpion has stung Marie-Y and sucks the poison from her wound. Seeing Oph naked reminds me of my nakedness. When I see Oph itching, my skin gets itchy.[16] I feel around in the closet for a pair of my own pants to get involved with.

---

[16] Inducing me to wake up.

Act V: Scene vi
Retrospect from the Clam Bed

INT. Studio de la Suture, Paris.
October 26, 2005. 3:03 p.m.

I wear Crawdaddy-O's claws to frame the shot, in the crescent-shaped vulva coffin, the mother of the flesh-colored prototype that I've been sleeping on every night. And now they're asking me to pretend to sleep in Spider-whore's clam bed. Despite the unrelenting light, I really do fall in and out of sleep, with a brooding guilt that I am only getting paid to *pretend to* sleep. Nobody notices me sleeping. The rest of the crew bicker incessantly and smoke cigarettes. I confide in Marie-Yves that I fell asleep and she says it's okay, "they know not the change in effect." So I allow myself to sleep on the set, except I keep waking myself with crazy dreams I feel guilty for having, especially when they are about Marie-Y and she is right there on this set with me.

Without my talkie-talkie on, I have no idea what they are saying. I can only imagine that it is about us—me and my brother Œuf, the "Américaines". I can listen in in English if I want but choose not to, thinking I may as well pick up some French. I listen for the word "Jaune" then take my position and wait around more.

In the lethargic timelessness of misunderstanding I sense an impending mutiny. In the excesses of catered creamy foods and Beaujolais we consume. Everybody is always waiting on someone or something, waiting and waiting—all for a few seconds of shooting. Marie-Y and the gaffer smell each other's armpits, first left then right, then they rub up and down on each other a few times. This is how people greet each other here. Men to women, women to women and men to men. Even if they just saw each other hours before. Even strangers. Even if they despise the person. From my perspective in the vulva clam bed, this smelling and rubbing ritual looks absurd. I'm embarrassed to partake. But when in Paris do as the Parisians. Œuf doesn't buy into it and shakes hands. He has a special "crawdad" handshake and insists on doing it to remain in character. I think it's more like a Spock handshake. It involves splaying your fingers in two pairs and spreading them wide, then slotting the V that forms into the recipient's V. Œuf always keeps his hands in V formation, even when he's acting as Troy. Bernard claims he stole this idea from Egon Schiele but is okay with it and agrees it fits Troy's character. It hints at his Crawdaddy-O yearnings.

Me, I just observe and take simple commands. I move my head to the side. I walk up to the red tape. I run away like I am being chased. If I'm asked, I pretend to sleep. I usually end up sleeping for real. I could probably fuck on demand if someone asked me to. I don't have a problem taking orders. There are lots of scenes of running, but nothing is chasing me and nothing is chasing Œuf when they actually do the shooting except the cameras. It is getting to the point where I can do all these required actions in my sleep—these actions that Œuf will eventually act out, for real.

Act III: Scene vii
Troy Becomes Crawdaddy-O

EXT. Night. Back Alley behind the Porkfish Belly.
Circa 2000.

The camera closes in on Troy, lying in a mangled heap in a pile of garbage. He is badly beaten. A rusty syringe is hanging out of his arm. He struggles to sit upright and take in his surroundings.

                                              Cut to:

Troy's p.o.v. shows blurred disorientation (and unsteady-camera work).[17] FOUR SAILORS circle around Troy, wiping off their hands.

                        SAILOR #1
                    (Spitting on Troy)
            Serves you right, punk!

They turn to leave the alley but get caught in an invisible web. CILIA THE SPIDER-WHORE pounces from a second story window, scampering down the web. She bundles them together, wrapping them in cobweb.

---

[17] Begin arthropodic trip.

Insert:

Silky thread spewing from a Black Widow's spinneret.[18]

Cut to:

The cocooned sailors wriggle to get free but are helpless.

Cut to:

Troy watching all of this in a daze, thankful but skeptical.

Cut to:

The spider-whore sucking the blood from one of the cocooned soldiers. When she finishes, she wipes her chin with one of her eight legs.

Insert:

Blood dribbling down Cilia's chin, her tongue lashing out to slurp it up. She turns towards Troy.

                    TROY
                 (terrified)
          What did you do to them?

Cilia pulls the needle out of Troy's arm.

                  SPIDER-WHORE
          I'm saving them for later. Question is,
          what to do with you? You've lost a lot
          of blood.

                    TROY
          Don't hurt ... me.

                  SPIDER-WHORE
          Don't worry. You're practically one of
          us already. All you need is some
          nourishment.

She scampers over to a cocooned sailor, sucks his blood, then returns to Troy. He is too weak to stop her. She grabs him by the chin, kisses him and spits the blood into his mouth.

---

[18] Stock footage.

Troy drinks and is revitalized. He gorges until he passes out. The spider-whore carries him up her web and into her chamber. She tends to his wounds.

MONTAGE[19]
- Meiosis, blood cells dividing
- Exoskeleton expanding, skin hardening
- Twitching, flexing muscles
- Connective tissue spreading

                                        Fade to black:

Beat.

                                        Fade in:

Troy comes to and is staring at Cilia who is no longer a spider-whore, but a beautiful woman.

                    TROY
                (still dazed)
        Where am I?

                    CILIA
        I'm Cilia. I've given you eternal life.

Cilia leans over to kiss Troy. He can't believe this is happening. Once he is over the initial shock, he closes his eyes and lets his hands roam over her body. After some time, he opens his eyes to discover his hand is in fact a claw, grasping at her cephalothorax. Before he has time to react, she pounces and straddles him with all eight legs. She strokes him delicately, milking silky threads from his nipples.

                    TROY
        I'm as open-minded as the next guy, but
        this is way too kinky for me.

                                        Insert flash:

Troy's eight-plated tail thrusts and curls, flapping wildly.

                    TROY
        What have I become?

---

[19] Stock footage.

                              CILIA
          You are Crawdaddy-O.

                                                 Flash On:

Creamy juices oozing out of a freshly squashed
cockroach, nanoseconds after it has been stepped on.[20]
Followed by a buzzing sound.

                                                 Cut to:

Pinocchio enters the room. He is a giant mosquito.

                                                 Cut to:

Crawdaddy-O and Cilia jump up.

                            PINOCCHIO
          Looky what the arachnio-slut caught in
          her cobweb tonight. A mud-sucking
          mooch! I thought you didn't want to
          partake?

Crawdaddy-O claws feebly at Pinocchio with little
success. Pinocchio breaks off his claws and throws
his body out the window.

                                                 Cut to:

Troy waking up in the same garbage heap at the end of
the alley. He examines himself—he is now entirely
human. But he is naked, lying crumpled in a pile of
garbage. A door opens and TWO CHEFS emerge, jabbering
in French. They take a garbage can full of discarded
seafood remnants and unknowingly dump it on Troy.

    "Cut!" yells Bernard through his talkie-talkie.
    Œuf spits out a mouthful of garbage. "Must we use the real
thing?"

---

[20] Stock footage.

                              104

Act III: Scene viii
Making Poisson Cru

INT. Day. Dream Sequence.
November 1, 2005. 1:44 p.m.

I woke up again in French Polynesia, only this time I was Œuf. I was free to do anything. I went into a bodega to get some sundries, but no one spoke English. I didn't know what to ask for or how to ask for it. I selected the following items off the shelf:

— 12 Eagle Claw® *crochets de poissons, taille 8* (imported from the U.S.)

— 25 meters of 7 kg *ligne opaque* (imported from France)

— 6-pac of Vahine® *bière* (local)

— 1-meter *baguette* (local)

— A postcard in English with a recipe for *Poisson Cru*

The front of the postcard (what caught my eye) had a picture of a three topless Tahitian nymphs chewing on fish. The back had the recipe for *Poisson Cru*, or Raw Fish:

Ingredients:

— 1 coconut

— 2 limes

— 1 red onion

— $\frac{1}{2}$ kg of taro root

— 4.5 mls of 20% ethyl acetate in iso-octane

— 1 cucumber

— 1 kg of yellowfin tuna

— grated key lime zest

— 2 μl 5x ligation buffer

— sea salt to taste

Methodology:

1. Poisson cru is not so much a linear recipe as an effervescent method of preparation.

2. To be true poisson cru, ingredients must not be purchased. Stealing is discouraged, but permitted.

3. Always start with freshly caught, still living, fish.

4. Cut the live fish into tongue-sized strips. Set aside.

5. Combine the rest of the ingredients in a wood bowl.

6. Deviations are encouraged depending on what's in season and readily available.

7. The resulting mixture must be chewed by menstruating virgins. (Salivary enzymes activate the true flavor of the fish.)

8. After fifteen minutes of steady chewing, mouthfuls are spit back in the bowl.

9. Centrifuge down and extract any undigested fibers. (These are toxic to most men.)

10. Add the fish, but not long enough for the lime and enzyme mixture to penetrate the fish and cook it. The surface should turn an opaque color, but the inside should remain raw.

11. Eat alone.

||: ||: ||: ||:

When I showed the Tahitian clerk the list of ingredients he pointed to where everything was and looked the other way. I helped myself. Finding the virgins would be problematic, but the methodology was vague enough that I could improvise.

I ventured out on a dock that appeared to be owned by no one. There were dolly tracks and tape marks on the dock like someone had been shooting a film from it. The lights were still set up, bathing the scene artificially. Otherwise there were no other signs of life besides some porkfishes jumping offshore. It was a little too early to be drinking beer, but I needed the can to spool the line on to catch my fish. I drank the beer and wound the line around the empty can. Then I tied the hook on the line and wadded up some bread, chewing on it briefly so it would stick to the hook.

Before I even got my line in the water, a redhead came swimming towards me on a surfboard. There were no waves so I'm not sure what the surfboard was good for. She came right for me and parked her board just below me on the dock. Her back was smooth and bronzed, uninterrupted by any tan lines. I would have said something, but the only French words I could think of were "poisson cru." I threw my hook in and waited.

After a while, she twisted supine. She wasn't wearing a top. She was a perfect specimen, though she couldn't have been more than fourteen so I felt guilty for thinking so. Even though there was no wind, her hair was flowing. She was bathed in the artificial light. It was all too perfect. Maybe she was the reason for the dolly tracks. I kept checking over my shoulder to see if it was a model shoot or a movie.

I reeled in my hook, spooling the line on the beer can. The doughy wad was gone. I hooked on another wad and threw it out. I wasn't feeling any bites. After a while, she sighed, flipped prone and said, "au revoir." Besides those parting words, no indication was given that I existed.

"I'm making poisson cru," I blurted, thinking she'd at least understand the last two words. But it was too late. As she was paddling away I noticed she didn't have two legs, but one tail fin. This whole time she had been a mermaid. To top it off, I only then remembered that I needed a menstruating virgin for my poisson cru recipe.[21] Not that I knew for a fact she was menstruating.[22] I literally kicked myself for not making the deduction, waking myself up. I was no longer Œuf or Oph, not even John or Jaune, but Stu. I was still fishing on the artificially lit dock with the dolly tracks and still had the poisson cru ingredients, minus the fish, which I had yet to catch. I wasn't certain

---

[21] By definition, all mermaids are virgins.
[22] See requirement 7 on page 106.

about the legitimacy of the mermaid though. I bent up from my supine position and tossed my line back in.

Eventually the redhead came strolling back out on the dock, except now she had legs and was fully clothed in a linen pantsuit. We instinctually smelled each other's armpits and rubbed against each other. Taking off her flip-flops, she sat down on the edge of the dock next to me. We couldn't really communicate, but from what I could gather she was Albert Camus' granddaughter. To make conversation, I asked her if she knew Marie-Yves Curie. She nodded vacantly. I went on speaking because it was more awkward not to, admitting that I hadn't read Camus, but knew of him through The Cure song. Through a walkie-talkie that materialized out of thin air, I started singing the lyrics: "standing on the beach/with a gun in my hand/staring at the sea/staring at the sand." She lit up. She had heard of The Cure. As I was singing into the reverb-laden walkie-talkie, I realized I must've been John after all, as Stuart didn't listen to The Cure. I was mad at John for inhabiting my dream. So I decided to "molt" John.

I wasn't sure how Camus' granddaughter would take it, so I said I was hot, took off my shirt and jumped in the water. I dove under to molt John. Opening my eyes underwater, I could see perfectly. I had a crawdad tail and claws. I felt guilty for having them. I was afraid to surface not knowing how Camus' granddaughter would take it. But at the same time I didn't want her to think I was drowning and then risk her life saving me. It was too late. I heard a splash as she dove in after me. She was back to being a mermaid. She swam up to me, close enough to tease me as my claw impulsively reached out to grab at her. Then I remembered Marie-Y and felt terrible even though nothing had happened either way. I kept telling myself I wasn't John or Œuf so it wouldn't be cheating even if something *did* happen. My claws kept snapping, but they were useless for grabbing a hold of anything as they were.

ACT IV

INT./EXT. Day. Sequential Montage Sequence
November 11, 2005. 4:20 p.m.

I do all the things that Œuf does, it's just never on film. At least not the edited final product. Sometimes when we watch the unedited dailies I see myself. When they are doing the clapperboard, or testing the lighting, it is me: Jaune, Yolk, Stu. I might end up on the cutting room floor but at least there is evidence of my existence, inside this studio. Outside the studio is a different story. The only time we ever see the sunlight is driving to and from Studio la Suture from Marie-Yves' habitation. I'm tanner than I was doing fieldwork in Georgia, and it's all from artificial light. The set lights keep my chigres hiding under my skin. Œuf's condition has worsened, though he still refuses to acknowledge that the fleshy horn on his forehead is more than a pimple. He keeps picking at it, making it worse. He blames the infected pimple on the red paint and all the make-up he must wear, and the antennae that are grafted to his head on a daily basis. He brings up the actress in *Goldfinger* every time — how she died after being covered in gold paint. And every time Marie-Y points out that this happened in the movie and Œuf insists it happened in real life while they were shooting the movie giving them the idea for the scene and Marie-Y points out that they obviously already had the idea for it because why else would they be covering her body in paint in the first place. Œuf digs himself in deeper and deeper. He continues to deny the growth on his forehead. His embarrassment is playing the role of anger. He channels his sensitivities into the hard exoskeleton characteristic of Crawdaddy-O. Œuf also reiterates that if one more person calls him Egg or Œuf he's walking off the set.

Deep down, I know what it's like to be Oph and feel confident I could take his place in a pinch. While he pretends to have sex with the actresses, I pretend to pretend over and over with their stand-ins. Whenever he has conflicts with men, it is me that takes the punches. My perspective to Oph is unique, not just because he is my brother. I could be him given the chance. Everyone on the set knows me as Œuf White's little brother, or Crawdaddy-

O's stand-in, or at best, Jaune. But I am actually in the film for a few stunts of my own. At least parts of me—a quick blur of my neck being bitten, my leather-chapped ass being lashed or an insert of my knuckles being stepped on. That was me, from behind, climbing the drainpipe in the alley. That was me, dressed as Crawdaddy-O, being heaved into the dumpster. And every time they cut the film and insert Troy or Crawdaddy-O as played by Œuf, who I know as my brother John. He's the one who gets up, brushes himself off and walks away.

Nothing is filmed in the order it happens in the script. Not only that, I'm the only one still grounded to the outside world—when I'm awake. Every time something out of the ordinary happens, every one consults their scripts to see if it *should be* happening. Even a rat that wandered onto the set one day causing a commotion—no one knew what to do until, waking up, I chopped his head off with the clapper. I didn't even have time to think about it.

Everything is non-sequential and resource dependent. It makes Marie-Y's life hell. And now the growth on Oph's forehead has thrown a wrench into the production schedule. Bernard has shifted around the close-up scenes with Troy to shoot later. Most of us are on the set sixteen hours a day. We have to constantly remind ourselves it's temporary. All people look forward to is the downtime after the shoot. Those that have been through this more than once tell us all we'll look forward to in the downtime is the next film. We communicate through talkie-talkies even when we are in the same room. Oph is always on the studio grounds but he's usually off in make-up, wardrobe, special effects or who knows where else. Half the time is spent tracking him down once the scene is set. And then once they find Œuf, they have to track down all the people that went looking for him, and by this time, the other actors are pissed off that they are waiting around, so they go off to take a break.[23]

On the schedule for today, Œuf[24] will solicit and inject narcotic bug juice, becoming Crawdaddy-O. Even though he, Troy, has

---

[23] Studio la Suture law requires all cast members to take a 5-minute break for every hour they work. "Work," as defined by the studio includes any time spent on the studio grounds. Break times need not coincide.

[24] Egg (Oph (John (Troy)))

111

already suffered the consequences (on camera) of being a crawdad, I'm not sure what the effects are on my brother. He blames his growth, amongst other things, on the crawdad costume elements.[25] The scene where he is being comforted then raped by Cilia the Spider-whore has already been shot. That scene happens chronologically after today's shoot—after being beaten up by the patriotic sailors. This shot is on location, in a real alley in Paris, though with all the lights and props, it feels like a studio. As I lay on the cold cobblestone, I keep myself busy imagining all the real shoes that have treaded here, polishing the cobblestone. Before the set dressers hosed it down and applied canned grit. Marie-Y is arranging the litter in the alley to match the last shot. She uses Polaroids for reference. I am laying supine in the fake garbage heap while they set up the shot. I fall asleep until Marie-Y wakes me. "Do you think me is a used being by Egg?" she asks through her talkie-talkie, even though I'm close enough to smell her diabetic breath. I spend more time on the set with Marie-Y than I do with Œuf. But all our conversations revolve around Œuf or the studio drama that inevitably centers on Œuf. He is the only topic we have in common.

"Being used for what?" I ask.

"For his girlfriend of Paris. I think not he respects I who am true." Marie-Yves adjusts some fake fish bones around my head.

"I am the one he doesn't have respect for," I say. "Just look at me. Over."

"This is not true," she says. "You owe it to see the manner in which he talks over you. He looks toward you in reality. Why is it you are here you think? He was excited how you came out. He lets you make his stunts for you to earn the stitches extra. Done."

The whistle sounds for the late morning coffee break.[26] Everyone congregates around the Kraft table, sniffing each other's armpits and rubbing against one another and smoking cigarettes. On the way there, some American tourists that breached security ask for my signature. They really ask for Oph's signature but Oph has authorized me to sign for him. For a moment I try to imagine what the Americans must think of all this. Then I take a step further back, wondering what another species from another

---

[25] As Oph mentions frequently, Studio la Suture also provides no health insurance, nor death or dismemberment.

[26] This is another stipulation, a national one, in addition to Studio la Suture's own 5-minute break per hour law.

112

planet would think if they came across this film shoot. I ask Marie-Yves, someone who has worked her whole adult life in film, to imagine what it would be like, to really put herself in alien shoes—those who have never seen nor heard of a film. "This is sucks, these hypothesis of yours," she says, thinking I am only pitching a hypothetical scenario for another film.

Act IV: Scene iii
Forage and Retreat

INT. Night. White's Residence, Savannah, GA.
January 6, 2006.

Crawfish (8:1)—To withdraw from an undertaker (informal).

—Idiom: "To stick in one's craw"
To cause abiding discontent and resentment:

> *"I dreamt that my cough was a mistake in the editing, and that by cutting, pasting and moving the cough I could sleep quietly . . . [The film] had killed me. It now rejected me and lived its own life. The only thing I could see in it were the memories attached to every foot of it and the suffering it had caused me."*[27]

Undertaker (6:6)—one whose business it is to undertake or make arrangements or to bind oneself to stick or plant another one's (molted) remnants into the ground:

> *We acted out scenarios on our mother's grave. Not that our mother had a tomb marking a particular spot—we let the mamnewts and crawdads loose on any tombstone we could find. The clean marble surface made for a good battlefield.*

‖:   ‖:   ‖: ‖: ‖:

---

[27] Jean Cocteau, *Beauty and the Beast: Diary of a Film*

Act IV: Scene iv
Pinocchio Dumps Troy into the Seine (Rehearsal)

EXT. Day. Bridge Over the River Seine, Paris.
November 3, 2005.

"Of agreement!" Bernard barks through the translating talkie-talkie. "Let's go to make this once more time. Begin the action a little back for that Our Mother is in the rear." This is the eighth time we've gone through this. The cameraman's assistant slaps some blue tape marks on the iron railing. The set dresser rips off the old marks. This is a real bridge, but to us it's a prop. There are real people that use this bridge to get to work, and now they have to go around. All for this.

Pinocchio's stand-in, Pascal, drives us back down to the bottom of the bridge in a black Range Rover. He doesn't speak English so there's not much to say. We sit in the car with our talkie-talkies simultaneously blaring orders, his in French, mine in English. We are waiting to run through the scene again with no film in the camera.

It's a long shot. They've closed off the whole bridge and then some. A crowd of spectators watches from behind a police line. The spectators, mostly American tourists, probably think I'm my brother Oph. They watch us for hours, waiting to witness something so they can say they saw it happen in real life.

[Time passes.]

Bernard gives the signal and I slump over in the backseat. We take off towards the bridge. I'm asleep before we even get there. The camera follows behind us in another car. Pinocchio's stand-in stops our car, runs around and pulls my sleeping body out the passenger side. When he pulls on my arms, they come off and he falls backwards, almost tumbling over the rail. I wake up with my arms intact. He tries again and I help so he is not carrying my full weight. In the real shot Pinocchio will carry Crawdaddy-O, much to Œuf's disgust (in real life, not the script). The camera car pulls past us and zooms in as Pascal pretends to drag me up to the rail. The boom mic operator jumps out and holds the microphone over us.

Just as I get up to the cast-iron rail I mechanically say, "remember I'm a crayfish, a bug that can breathe water."

114

To which Pascal responds in incomprehensible English, "you, my friend, are a dead man."

I can smell Pascal's cologne. And he really milks every word though there's no film in the camera. He was Bernard's doorman before this and now he's an aspiring actor who hands around his airbrushed headshot to everyone on the set. Bernard yells, "stop" and Pinocchio's stand-in lets go of me.[28]

Bernard barks more orders through his talkie-talkie. They drive the car back down and beyond where we started. Pinocchio and Crawdaddy-O will drive faster on the real take.

[Time passes.]

[In the insert shot it is cloudy and now the sky is blue. We are waiting for sufficient clouds to build up.]

[Time passes.]

Marie-Yves and I are sent to fetch Œuf. He is in a trailer parked at the end of the bridge smoking hash with Élodée, the make-up artist that used to be his personal assistant. Marie-Yves and Élodée smell each other's armpits and rub against each other. Élodée does not acknowledge me, even after I thank her again for making the travel arrangements to get me here.

> MARIE-YVES
> I see, this is what it is you do out here.

> ŒUF
> You guys want to partake?

> MARIE-YVES
> You are not funny. Everybody waits for Troy.

> ŒUF
> Let them wait. Troy's got to get in the right frame of mind.

---

[28] The second unit has already filmed the insert shot—the dummy falling off the bridge. We already saw it in the rushes the night before—a 2-second clip of a Crawdaddy-O doll (that looked totally fake) falling from the bridge. And we already filmed the scene where two porkfishes rescue Crawdaddy-O.

115

MARIE-YVES

It is enough cloudy to go. This is
sucks.

ŒUF

You can't force these things. Look at
these claws?
(flails claws in air)
These aren't easy to swallow.

MARIE-YVES

The costume artist did make them not
for to handle a hash pipe. These are
special claws for detachment.

ŒUF

. That's what make-up artists are for.
*(leans over as ÉLODÉE lights his
pipe and sticks it in his mouth)*

MARIE-YVES

You just like her because she does not
speak the English—

ŒUF

(interrupting)
Oph just likes her name. *Élodée.* In
English it's a type of seaweed.

MARIE-YVES

—and she is the *assistant* to the make-
up artist.

ŒUF

Lighten up. We're just trying to have
some fun here. You want to try some of
this, Jaune?
*(doesn't give Jaune time enough
to respond)*
Here, Élodée, give my little brother a
hit.

Élodée shrugs, lights the pipe and holds it out into
the empty air.[29] Élodée notices but reacts
nonchalantly to Jaune's luminous presence.

---

[29] SPFX: Smoke travels through Jaune, giving the illusion of a smoke-filled glass
chamber. He is illuminated from the inside.

                         ŒUF
How can you take any of this shit
seriously? Look at this-
                    (holds up claws)
These look like potholders you'd get at
a cracker barrel. And this tail-
                    (shows tail)
it's skinny and barbed like a devil's
tail you'd see in comic books. Or did
crawdad get translated to *scorpion* when
they   gave   the   description   to   the
costume department?

                    MARIE-YVES
          *(flipping earnestly through
            her dog-eared script)*
This is the point. Bernard is a, how
do you say, dada surréaliste.

                         ŒUF
That   is   a   weak   justification   for
sucking. I'm ashamed to have my name on
this   film.   I   should've   used   a
pseudonym.

                        JAUNE
You did. You are Oph White, twice, or
rather, thrice removed.

                         ŒUF
Thrice removed from what?

                        JAUNE
Thrice removed from the name our mother
and father gave you.

                         ŒUF
That's one way to think about it.
     *(takes another hit from the hash
     pipe that Élodée lights for him)*
Or you can think of me as an extension.
A progressive evolution from the swampy
depths   that   spawned   us.   Phylogeny
recapitulating ontogeny.

                        JAUNE
Way to bite the hand that feeds.

                         117

ŒUF

Feeds us what? Catfish and grits?

MARIE-YVES

This is good. I've not heard you two
discourse over your parental beings.

ŒUF

What's to say? Our mother was
hysterical.

MARIE-YVES

Hysterical, like funny?

ŒUF

We're talking clinical hysteria. Not
funny. Bad crazy, and a lush to boot.
She was completely out of touch with
the world. And all our father did was
tiptoe around the pedestal he put her
on.

JAUNE

Why do you speak of him in the past
tense?

ŒUF

He still does, even with her dead.

JAUNE

Regardless, they brought you into this
world.

ŒUF

Anybody can have babies. It's not
rocket science. It's another thing to
make something of your life. I made me
who I am. I have nothing to do with
them.
        (claps his claws together)
Matter of fact, everyone needs to call
me Troy going forward. That's all I am
while I'm here. *Troy.* If anyone calls
me Egg or Oph or especially John, I'm
walking. Got it? Élodée? *Je ma pell
Troy. No pas Œuf.*

Élodée nods and taps the pipe to knock the residuals
out. Troy motions to his head and Élodée sets to work
reattaching his antennae.

                           JAUNE
          Regardless of what we call you, you
          need to chill out or you're gonna end
          up like our mother.

                           TROY
                 (exhales a cloud of smoke)
          What do you think I'm smoking here?
          Crack, like Big Bubba? That dude's out
          of control. Did you see the way Bernard
          scrapped the catacomb scenes because of
          that claustrophobic crackhead?

                        MARIE-YVES
          They were with water flooded.

                           TROY
          I haven't seen it rain since we've been
          here.

                           JAUNE
          That's because we're always here in the
          studio. Might do us some good to take a
          day or two off.

                           TROY
          Is that the thanks we get for taking
          you to the Pompidou center last
          weekend?

                           JAUNE
          We only went there because there was an
          exhibit on the history of French film.
          You used everything as a springboard to
          vent about Bernard and the rest of the
          crew. You need to get your mind off
          movies altogether. And your, thing-
                    (points to growth on Troy's
                            forehead)
          It's oozing pretty bad.

Élodée grabs a tissue and dabs at Troy's growth,
which by now is protruding over an inch from his
forehead.

                           TROY
          Damn it to hell. It's all this makeup.

Élodée gobs more paste on it.

                            119

                         JAUNE
          That's not make-up. That's reality.

                       MARIE-YVES
          You owe it to yourself to arrange for a
          doctor to look, Œuf, it's disgusting
          really.

                         TROY
          Damn it! I told you not to call me Œuf.
          I'm Troy. Get it through your head. If
          you don't like me as Troy, here's the
          door.
                    (kicks the door open)

                                        Flash on:

          Tourists clustering on the other side of the door
          trying to sneak a peak and take pictures before it
          swings back shut.

                       MARIE-YVES
          You are that which is in my habitation
          living.

                         TROY
          Is that the way it is? Do you think
          Troy's using you for your habitat?
                    *(Élodée swivels his head back
                    into position, instructing him
                         to hold still)*
          You know, Troy's been thinking. Why do
          we even go "home" at all?
                    *(attempts to make quote signs with
                    claws when he says "home")*
          If we can even call your habitation
          that. Troy spends hours each night
          getting all this makeup off, just to go
          to your habitation to sleep so we can
          wake up and come here to put it all
          back on again. We may as well just stay
          here and never get out of costume.

                       MARIE-YVES
          Have it your way.

          Marie-Y exits trailer, parting the flock of autograph
          seeking tourists.

                         120

Flash on:

S-shaped trail of slime in her wake.

Aerial shot on:

Outside of trailer, parked at the head of the bridge, a bustling tourist attraction made even more chaotic by the presence of the film crew.

Back to:

The silent make-up trailer.

                    JAUNE
          Everybody's waiting.

                         TROY
          For what?

                         JAUNE
          For you. Troy.

Élodée lines up Troy's face to inspect it.

                         TROY
          Pigpussy is just jealous that Troy
          spends so much time with Élodée, but
          what can Troy say? We have our jobs to
          do.
                    (takes hit off pipe)
          Speaking of jobs, this is funny and
          true. My friend was working on some
          film with Sylvester Stallone and Sly
          went off with an extra to his trailer
          to get a blowjob during his lunch break.

                         JAUNE
          We should really get going.

                         TROY
                    (exhaling)
          But he forgots to turn his mic off so the
          whole crew could hear everything he was
          saying. They amplified it over the
          loudspeakers. Supposedly he kept saying,
          *take the shaft, cradle the balls. Take
          the shaft, cradle the balls*, over and
          over.

Élodée smirks at the protuberant growth on his forehead, which is oozing through the make-up. She throws up her arms in frustration.

On the table in front of Troy is an EARMARKED BOOK ON BIOLOGICAL MORPHOLOGY. He struggles to pick it up with his claws.

                              TROY
                  (sighing, thumbing through the book)
              Troy needs to just go with this thing.
              Work it into his character.

Jaune takes the book from his hands to help him. Flips through indiscriminately. Goes to a section on OCEANIC FORMS. Hones in on a sub-section: DEEP SEA CREATURES.

Montage:
- bioluminescent jellyfish
- white ghost shrimp
- pork-fish
- hydrothermal vents spewing mineral laden water
- deep-sea anglerfish

Troy looks over his shoulder.

                              JAUNE
              There! This one.
                  (points to the DEEP SEA ANGLERFISH)
              This is totally you. At least for the
              time being.

Abandoned in Notre Dame

INT. White's Residence, Savannah, GA
January 8, 2006.

Hys•ter•i•a (his-'ter-E-&, -'tir-) *n.*
Psychoneurosis characterized by the manifestation of a detached physical ailment without an organic cause, such as sleepwalking, amnesia, episodes of hallucinations and other mental and behavioral aberrations. From Latin *hystericus*, hysterical, from Greek *husterikos*, from *hustero*, womb or "wandering womb" (from the former Freudian idea that disturbances in the womb caused hysteria). Hysteria is caused by a frustrated propagation of fictitious lies and can only be relieved by a cathartic reactivation of the primordial memory. The morphogenesis of hysterical expression hinges on the concept of dissociation or detachment. Proneness to severing into an ego-alien body may be in part genetic. A dead give-away is the "glove and stocking" distribution of motor disturbances that affect the limbs whereby identity is attached to a body-image concept with additional appendages that render them incapable of coping with past trauma (perhaps the intent).

Hys•ter•i•cal (his-'ter-i-k&l) *adj.*
Extremely funny, for the time being.

Act IV: Scene vi
Pinocchio Dumps Troy into the Seine (for Real)

EXT. Day. Bridge Over the River Seine, Paris.
November 3, 2005.

                                        Flash on:

Troy, emerging from his trailer in full Crawdaddy-O
regalia, with the addition of A FLESHY ANGLERFISH
EXTENSION [SPFX] hooking six inches out from his
forehead.

The costume artist, SOPHIE, grabs his barbed tail to
keep it from dragging on the ground. A flock of
awaiting fans ask Troy for his autograph. He
dismisses them with a wave of his claw.

                    JAUNE
          Get a clue people. I'd like to see you
          sign autographs with claws.

                    TOURIST
          Who are you?

                    JAUNE
          Jaune.

                    TOURIST
          Yah, but who are you in real life?

                    JAUNE
          I'm Oph's brother and stand-in.

                    TOURIST
          Can we have your autograph?

                                        Flash to:

Big Bubba Bixon, emerges from his trailer, with the
headmask for his Pinocchio costume tucked under his
arm. Takes a swig of his bottled water. The tourists
flock over in his direction to seek his autograph. He
stops to sign some.

                    TROY
          What an amateur.

Jaune takes charge and guides Troy through the crowd like Crawdaddy-O is a prizefighter making his way to the ring.

>   JAUNE
>   Don't worry about that pinhead! Focus.
>   You are Crawdaddy-O. Channel it!

Cut to:

The rest of the crew stand around smoking and making snide remarks under their breath. The ones that haven't seen each other in a while sniff each other's armpits and rub against one another. Bernard goes over the logistics of the scene to a bored and frustrated Troy. Bernard doesn't notice his dangling phalangocyte until he's been talking to him for a few minutes.

>   BERNARD
>   What is this?

Flash on:

Bernard flicks the appendage and it pendulums back and forth.

>   TROY
>   It's Crawdaddy-O's lure.

>   BERNARD
>   This is not in the script.
>   *(into talkie-talkie)*
>   Sophie, get this off of Egg. It should
>   not be there. Done.

>   SOPHIE'S VOICE
>   *(through talkie-talkie)*
>   No, this is my department not. Egg's
>   face is owned by makeup. Done.

>   TROY
>   And just so you know, my name is Troy.
>   I don't want to be called Œuf or Egg.

>   BERNARD
>   *(directly)*
>   *Élodée, obtiennent cette chose outre de*
>   *son visage.*

                    ÉLODÉE
                   (shrugs)
        C'est special effects.

                     TROY
        This is my face. I can do what I want
        with it.

                    BERNARD
        This is not your face. This is
        Crawdaddy-O's face. Crawdaddy-O has not
        a, a thing, coming from his face.

                     TROY
        Open your mind. Think of it as an extra
        antennae that he uses to lure his prey.

Bernard grabs at Troy's lure, and Troy knee-jerks
back at him, mouth wide open, narrowly missing.

                    BERNARD
        Are you crazy, American?

                     TROY
        If the lure goes, I go.

                                              Cut to:

Big Bubba, already in the driver's seat of the Range
Rover, engine running. He dons his head mask and
mosquito nose, undergoing the transformation to
Pinocchio.

                    BERNARD
               (looking at his watch)
        D'accord. We no see this thing not in
        this scene. Allez!
                 *(yells instructions into his
                   talkie-talkie.)*

Troy reluctantly gets into the back of the Range
Rover.

Montage:
- Blue sky.
- Crew standing around looking up, waiting for clouds
to roll in.
- Gaffers fix a bulb that has gone out.
- Pinocchio and Crawdaddy-O wait in the car looking
pissed off, even through their costumes.

                      126

- Tourists and onlookers watch intently as the crew stands around doing nothing.
- Jaune sleeps, his eyes fluttering in R.E.M.
- Clouds finally roll in.

>   BERNARD
>   (via talkie-talkie)
>   Of agreement. Let us roll the film.

The cameraman's assistant claps the clapperboard.

>   BERNARD
>   Action!

A dominoed hush overtakes the crowd of onlookers, propagated by a half-dozen strategically placed production assistants. The assistant to the A.D. gives Pinocchio the signal and he peels out, the camera car in hot pursuit. Everything is more or less like what Pascal and I did, but with more intensity.[30] The camera tracks the black Range Rover as it skids around the corner leading to the bridge. Pinocchio pulls up to the middle of the bridge, screeches on the brakes and jumps out.[31] Pinocchio runs around to the passenger side of the Range Rover. The car starts rolling backwards with Crawdaddy-O in the backseat. Bernard and Marie-Yves consult their scripts to see if this should be happening. When Troy feels the car roll, he bolts upright. Pinocchio rips off his head mask and mosquito nose and gives chase like a catcher after a foul ball. The boom mic operator jumps out of the way, dropping the microphone. The Range Rover plows through the parting crew, who drop everything and run for cover. The out-of-control car picks up speed and snags on various cables, pulling over some lights and tearing up the dolly tracks. It swerves and fishtails as Troy tries to jump out of the backseat and into the front. He is having difficulty grabbing the wheel with his crawdad mitts. The Range Rover coasts down the bridge and takes up the lighting shields at the corner then jumps a curb and careens off the marble façade of a bank building, loses speed and rolls through a crowd of screaming spectators until a calm bystander jumps in the front seat and pulls the emergency brake.

---

[30] Actually, a rather over-exaggerated, melodramatic effort if you ask me.
[31] I never understand why he is in such a hurry to dump my brother off the bridge.

Troy jumps out and stomps back up the bridge, flailing his crawdad mitts. One of the tourists, apparently thinking this was how the scene was supposed to happen, applauds. Then everyone applauds. A few hold out paper and a pen, asking for Troy's autograph. Troy shoves them aside. Big Bubba puffs up his costumed chest as Troy approaches. "You alright?" asks Big Bubba.

Troy ignores him, spitting on the ground as he walks past. "I hope you got all that," he says to Bernard. He throws his crawdad mitts to the ground. "Because I ain't doing that again. Crawdaddy-O's not setting foot in that car with this oaf."

"I pulled the safety brake," says Big Bubba, "It wasn't my fault."

Troy doesn't even look at Big Bubba. He is fixated on Bernard who is in turn fixated on Troy's phalangocyte, licking his lips.

"The guy's a porn star for fuck sake," says Troy. "Not the sharpest tool in the shed. But I guess you knew that all along."

"Hey man," says Big Bubba, "no need to get personal."

"Crawdaddy-O's done here," says Troy, kicking his discarded crawdad mitts and stomping back to his trailer.

Bernard, trying to be calm and collected, gathers up the loose pages of his script. "Of agreement," he mumbles into his talkie-talkie. "We can work with this. Conflict natural is good. We captured fine the part where they are driving on the bridge."

The crew resumes standing around waiting for the next scene.

Act IV: Scene vii
Grinding the Chariot of Desecration

EXT. Day/Night. Dream Sequence
November 4, 2005.

True to Troy's word, we call him Troy and we sleep on the studio grounds, which on this particular day happens to be the *place* Troy, circa 12th century B.C. At least this is where "I" wake up. We are in the shade of a drooping live oak tree in the Bonaventura cemetery in Savannah. At least Troy is. I'm knee-deep in a faux swamp. The banks look more like slabs of raw meat and the "grass" leading down to the swamp looks like shag carpet made of pubic hair. Our father is here, or at least he's giving me visual cues through a walkie-talkie so I know he must be nearby. Marie-Yves is also here, sitting with Troy under the tree. I think to introduce her to our father, but can't get a visual on him. Through the walkie-talkie I ask him for his coordinates but he only responds to tell me which relative direction I need to go. The "G" monument, as he calls it, is made of concrete but the core is steel rebar, so he has given me a metal detector to locate it.[32]

While all this is happening, Troy is narrating, explaining to Marie-Y what is going on as if what we are doing is a form of sign language and he is translating for her. He is speaking through a walkie-talkie that is being amplified over "Statichoey" brand loudspeakers that sound like what they are. "This is the part where Yolk gets bitten by a water moccasin," announces Troy, "though he doesn't know it yet."

"What is it, one water moccasin?" asks Marie-Y.

"A moccasin is a type of shoe worn by the peoples native to this region and, well, you know what water is so you can put the rest together. But all you need to know is that it is a species of snake."

Marie-Y is taking notes. She pulls a sequence of Polaroid snapshots out of her marsupial pouch[33] and lays them out. They show the swamp I'm standing in at prior times. "This won't work," she says. "Before we were here, this wasn't even a swamp, see?"

She shows Troy, but he doesn't even look. "That's the whole point. The water has risen since then. That's why they can't find the G-monument."

Even though I hear Troy say I'm going to be bitten by a snake, I realize there's nothing I can do except act surprised. A blue-ish gray snake grabs a hold of my pant leg and even though I'm expecting it, it scares me for real, and my scream of horror sounds genuine. Instinctually, I hack at the snake with my bush-axe. Despite what Troy has said, the snake has not broken my skin, so technically it didn't bite me. But that doesn't mean it still couldn't bite me. Hacking the snake in half, it becomes two snakes, both with heads and tails. I hack again and it becomes three snakes. Our father is yelling at me to stop, that I'm making matters worse. He goes back to his truck to get his .38 caliber. Troy comments to Marie-Y (as an aside), "that's the kind of man he was," speaking about him in the past tense though he's here with us.

As I'm waiting motionless, I notice that Élodée, the assistant to the makeup artist, is here, lying just under the surface of the

---

[32] It is submerged.
[33] I still don't consciously know about it.

water at my feet. She is completely naked with her red hair flowing in the tide. Her pubic mound is also red, verifying what Troy told me.[34] And her skin is green, though it might be on account of seeing her through the murky water. Because of the angle,[35] and the reflection on the surface of the water, I am the only one that can see her. I want to tell Troy, but Marie-Y is here and will get jealous. When I look again, Élodée flips prone and swims away.

Our father's truck is actually the Range Rover where Troy had his resignation inducing mishap the day before. And we are no longer in Savannah but under the same bridge over the river Seine where we were filming the day before. Our father returns with his gun.

"You can't shoot a snake with a gun," I say.

He winks at me and loads silver bullets into it. "Just you watch me."

Instead of aiming at the snake, or snakes, our father aims straight up into the sky, presumably to fire a warning shot. Marie-Y comments that in the scene before there were clouds, so it won't make sense.

While this is going on, a second unit is filming on the nearby steps of Notre Dame. It is a simple insert shot whereby a baby[36] is dropped off on the steps of Notre Dame. We don't see who it is dropping the dead fish/baby off, but we presume it is Troy. The dead fish/baby is his younger brother, *our* younger brother that was born right before our mother died. The responsibility had been bestowed on him to care for the child, though he neglected to tell us about it, keeping the dead fish/baby a secret this whole time. The burden was too much for him to handle on his own, so he bundled the dead fish/baby up to leave in the custody of the parish of Notre Dame. We all know this now, after the fact, because Troy is reading to us from the script, while he had effectively pushed the pause button on our father.

When he is done speaking, he releases the pause button and our father shoots his gun. We don't see where the bullet lands, but Troy tells us the bullet just happens to hit the dead fish/baby

---

[34] "The carpet matches the drapes."

[35] The duration of the sin of the angle of coincidence is proportional to the duration of the sin of retaliation in the unscripted media, or equivalently to the inverted duration of the indices of recombination. This follows from Fermat's principle of least time.

[36] To the audience, it is a baby wrapped in a blanket, but on the set we actually used a dead fish wrapped in newspaper.

as he places it on the steps. He says this to us as an aside — special insider knowledge read like commentary on the director's cut. When our father overhears this, he hangs his head low and walks into the river.[37]

"How is this possible?" asked Marie-Y.

"Our father has a built-in tracking device that enables him to detect minute variations in the Earth's magnetic field," Troy said, "but we're getting off track here. That's real life, that's not what's happening in the movie." Troy continues reading from the script. "Insulted after a dispute with Agamemnon, Achilles, our father, the greatest of the Argive warriors, withdraws in anger from the combat and sulks in his tent." Troy takes a crawdad and places it under a magnolia leaf. We are back in the shade of the huge live oak, all three of us, lounging on the pubic shag carpet. It is not Savannah, but a supposed recreation of Savannah, down to the hot and humid air they are pumping in.[38]

"During his absence," Troy continues, "the Trojan armies are successful and nearly capture the Achaean ships. The unborn child of Patroclus, the closest and dearest friend of Achilles, is killed by Hector. Seeking revenge, Achilles returns to the war and kills Hector.[39]"

"All the Argives run up to view the body of the dead Trojan leader. Many jest at and stab the corpse. Achilles strips the shell from Hector and fastens the naked body to his chariot by its segmented tail.[40] Then he gallops off, dragging Hector's corpse in great disgrace behind him."

I wake up in a sweat, not from being in the heat of Savannah, but from the heat of the artificial lights. It takes my eyes a minute to adjust. Then I remember we are filming the scene where Troy, half-dead, is dropped off on the steps of the Notre Dame. Before the priest discovers the body[41] unknown forces conspire to drag him away. This is the scene we have been preparing for.

---

[37] Evidently, as Troy told us, he walked underwater, along the Seine, under the Atlantic, and back to our home in Savannah.

[38] Which is putting me to sleep, though I am acutely aware that I am already sleeping.

[39] In real life the crawdad we called Hector was winning so we had to help Achilles out by dismembering Hector.

[40] The crawdad is still alive after Troy removes the shell.

[41] Which although is bundled to look like a baby, is really a fish.

131

Act IV: Scene viii
Defining Our Reproduction Habits

INT. Night. White's Residence, Savannah, GA
January 9, 2006.

Ang•ler•fish (ángglêrfish) *n.*

Bony bottom-dwelling fishes of the order *Lopohiiformes* named for their novel form of predation whereby a fleshy growth protruding from their forehead acts as a lure. The protruding lure (the *phalangocyte*) is actually a modified dorsal spine with a hook that is often shaped to mimic a small marine organism, or that can even ooze tempting secretions. In some deepwater species, the phalangocyte has a light-emitting or bioluminescent organ on the tip. The phalangocyte protrudes from between the fish's eyes, and terminates in an irregular growth of flesh (the s-cape) at the tip. The s-cape is moveable, and can be wiggled to simulate wounded prey, acting as bait. Its wide jaws, which extend all around the anterior circumference of the head, are wired to involuntarily trigger open with any contact to the s-cape. The anglerfish is able to dislocate and distend both its jaw and stomach, allowing it to swallow prey up to twice its size. The foreskin of the Anglerfish can host fringed appendages resembling fronds of seaweed. The anglerfish is able to assimilate the color and patterns on its body to match the surrounding seabed.

At birth, male anglerfish are equipped with well-developed olfactory organs. They have no digestive system and are not able to feed on their own recognizance. They must find a female anglerfish or they will die. Their hypersensitive olfactory organs enable them to detect the pheromones that signal the presence of female. When he finds a female, the male bites into her flank, releasing an enzyme which digests the skin of his own mouth and her body, fusing the pair down to the blood vessel level, becoming one.[42] Once he finds and attaches himself to a female, the male of the species then atrophies into nothing more than a pair of gonads that release sperm in response to hormonal triggers in the female's bloodstream that indicate an egg's release.

---

[42] The tail meat of the genus *Lophius* (also known as goosefish or monkfish) is used in Cajun cooking and is often compared to lobster tail in taste and texture, giving it the name "poor boy's lobster."

Act IV: Scene ix
Recouping Foreign-Antibodies

INT. Hôpital la Suture, Paris.
November 9, 2005. 12:13 p.m.

I'm writing this by the operating lights in the rehabilitation ward. The studio actually has this hospital on premises, a real functioning one that also doubles as a stage set where they shoot the French equivalent of E.R. and other movies that require hospital scenes. It's for the most part vacant when they're not shooting, but they keep a barebones staff that maintains the hospital in a functional dormancy to give it an air of legitimacy. There's a scene from the movie we are shooting here later on, but Jaune's current convalescence was not scripted.

Last thing I remember, we were having a "last supper," as Troy dramatically called it. Bernard's talkie-talkie translated it as an "intervention." He was forcing us all to sit down together at the same table—Troy, Bubba, the whole crew, all out of character, acting themselves. Bernard thought it would be good to step out of our roles and get to know each other as "natural beings."

Troy's phalangocyte had reached its full swollen length, dangling six inches out from his forehead. No one could keep their eyes off it, but no one dared bring it up. Troy was open about it, made snide jokes even. The phalangocyte and the tension between Troy and Bubba were occupying everyone's minds, including my own. To the extent that I had been neglecting what Jaune was telling me. It could've been any number of things that led to Jaune's illness:

1. Steak tartar. Essentially a raw mound of hamburger meat with a quail egg mixed in.
2. Cheese with mold all over it, though they insisted it was okay to eat.
3. A salad of dandelion greens picked from the studio grounds.
4. Snails.
5. Tuna salad with a written disclaimer: "Not Porkfish Safe."

These were all things I felt obligated to eat, along with a bunch of unidentifiable creamy dishes of various bruised shades of orange and purple. I tried to wash the accumulating taste down with wine, and:

6. My wine glass was perpetually refilling.
7. The *idea* of any of the above, juxtaposed with my *obligation* to eat them.

There were more familiar items, like French fries, but by the time the plate got to Jaune it was always empty. Everyone kept saying I could eat French fries at home, why not try something new, experience the real Paris? They thought I was being funny when I questioned whether the studio food represented real Parisian cuisine, chattering smugly amongst themselves in French. I should have known Jaune was sick when people commented that I was turning yellow. But they didn't seem too concerned. They said it fit my name. Troy slapped Jaune's back and said I was, "living up to my reputation." I checked Jaune's reflection in the window and couldn't see myself though I could see everyone else.

There was an empty space sitting between Troy and Marie-Yves, presumably Jaune. Bubba had been placed next to Troy on the other side of him to his left, and Bernard next to Bubba, even further left. Élodée was sitting next to Marie-Y on her right. This was all calculated by Bernard. He even took away our talkie-talkies so we had to communicate directly with each other. There were name cards on our plates when we went to sit down (after cocktails in the studio bar that began at exactly 13:75[43]). Even though Bubba was next to Troy, he kept talking to Jaune, around or through Troy. As Jaune was talking to him, all I could think about was Big Bubba as a porn star and how he must've looked in his movies. I can't remember what we were talking about—he was asking Jaune what it was like to grow up with Troy, and I was telling him how Troy (or John, as I called him) was into movies from the day he was old enough to hold a camera. I told him about *The Man Who Could Not Die*[44] and about the time we threw a dummy off a bridge into the Savannah River causing a fatal boat accident. Because we had used some of our own junk mail to stuff the dummy the Coast Guard found out who we were and our father took John's camera away, which is what prompted John to run away to Hollywood.

"Who's John?" asked Bubba.

---

[43] The studio had it's own system of time.
[44] See page 88.

"John is Troy," I said. I wasn't really all there and felt weird that Jaune was the one telling the stories about Troy while Troy just sat there drinking and listening, glad for once to not have the attention on him and his phalangocyte. Since Troy was between Bubba and Jaune, we had to keep leaning either way to talk in front of or behind him, depending on whether Troy was learning forward to take a bite or sip his wine.

After a while I discovered Jaune could see through Troy. At first he was made of a frosted glass and everything was blurry through him, but as my eyes adjusted he was clearly becoming translucent. I don't think it was just Jaune that had this ability to see right through him, as both Bubba and Bernard were looking directly back at me through Troy, so obviously it had something to do with Troy's physical appearance. With this realization, I started to feel more and more detached, to the point where I was watching Jaune's mouth talking, as "I" drifted away. At first it was euphoric, but then it became a struggle to stay involved in the conversation and I could tell people were noticing Jaune wasn't all there and I started to panic and sweat and get flushed, becoming hyper-sensitive to Jaune's waxing visibility in contrast to Troy's waning invisibility. Jaune still had Bubba fooled, who was laughing and I remember him saying, "I can't believe you two came from the same mother. It's like night and day." I wasn't seeing Bubba as Big Bubba anymore, but as Pinocchio, and when I looked at Troy, despite his transparency and his phalangocyte, he was Crawdaddy-O. Marie-Y was herself and she was sensing that something was wrong with Jaune, asking if I was okay, and Jaune kept saying yes, and not to worry, and she said I looked sick, "*really* yellow, jaundiced." Supposedly Jaune said he just needed some fresh air and to be alone, but I don't remember much beyond that point. Evidently, Jaune got up and went outside into a light drizzle. Troy and Marie-Y both started to get up to see if Jaune was okay, but Bernard yelled at them to leave me alone, that I was okay and clearly wanted to be alone, and not to be distracted from the business at hand, that we had an agenda to stick to that didn't necessarily include Jaune. Troy and Marie-Y said Jaune looked fine and I myself had told them not to worry and to go back inside and they did. Then Bernard put down his napkin and came outside into the rain. He said he wanted a word with me. He looked Jaune in the eye and said, "it promotes one to cross the wide moat. Purse severance promotion." At the time I had no idea what he meant by it. That was the last thing I remember.

When they found Jaune, I was in the vulva bed wearing Crawdaddy-O's outfit. I had thrown up all over myself and was mumbling that I had "swallowed pieces of our mother" and was "burning from the inside." According to Troy, Jaune was ranting on about "the changes going on inside of me," that whatever was incubating was now hatching, and when they took Jaune across the street to the studio hospital, I insisted I "could explain everything," that it was all on account of a case of chigres Stu brought from Georgia, and that no, chigres were not sexually transmitted.[45] The French doctors asked who Stu was and looked up chigres in their medical dictionary, but I told them it wouldn't do any good, that these chigres had mutated into an internal form[46] and now the chigres had succeeded in penetrating my stomach lining and into my blood system, inducing a sort of internal reconstitution.

   When they pumped Jaune's stomach they found no signs of chigres like I told them they wouldn't since the chigres had gotten into my blood. According to Marie-Y, these doctors, who were also bona fide actors, had determined my sickness was caused by tainted shellfish, even though we had not eaten any recently. But Marie-Y didn't look so sure, and admitted there wasn't a direct English translation for what they found. When they did an ultrasound, Marie-Y translated their findings by saying they found "your mother's womb inside you," an expression the French used to categorize a rare autoimmune disorder. In laymen's terms, they told me Jaune was rejecting specialized vestigial organs that had grown inside of me,[47] but that it was good, that he was rejecting them for a reason and that Jaune just needed to get rest and remain in a sterile environment as I was susceptible during this time. Eventually Jaune would void these vestigial organs and be better than new.

---

[45] Not that Jaune or Stu had had sexual relations since being in France.

[46] After all, our skin was a uniform organ that extended inside of us to our digestive tracts.

[47] To further complicate matters, Troy was trying to tell the doctors I had given him his liver. Fortunately they weren't paying attention to him. I can't substantiate this claim now. I have found no medical records regarding a liver transplant and our father knew nothing of the sort.

Act V

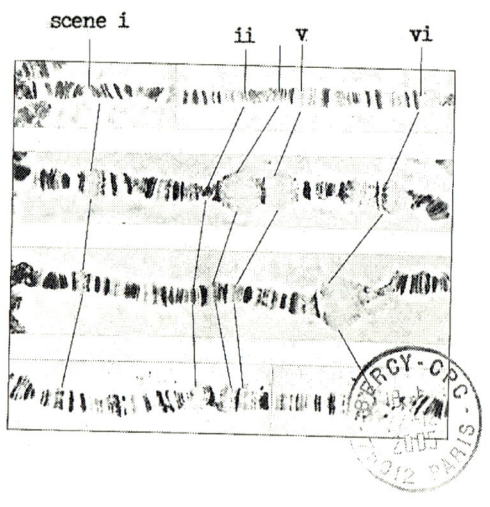

Act V: Scene i
Siren Reel

EXT. Day. Banks of the River Seine, Paris.
circa 2000.

A YOUNG BOY and his PIG-FACED MOTHER are fishing from
a bridge in front of the Notre Dame. The bridge is
rimmed with hanging moss in the shape of a moustache.
The banks of the river Seine are also turfed in hair-
like moss, sprouting from the grooves in the raw meat.
The son is on his tiptoes looking down into the water.
The pig-faced mother is looking off into the sky at
the flying buttresses supporting the church.

                         SON
          Who's gonna support us now that daddy's
          gone?

                    PIG-FACED MOTHER
          Fish on, son.

                                        Flash on:

Red and white bobber swirling in the eddy currents.

                                         Cut to:

Pig-faced mother staring at the bobber and the
surface, BLURRING OUT. BLUR IN to harsh light of an
operating room. Pig-faced mother emitting a deafening
squeal. Camera zooms into her pig-mouth, focusing on
a dangling tonsil, vibrating with the scream.

                                         Cut to:

Pig-faced mother in a gown on an operating table,
legs spread and sweating. Doctors and nurses scurry
every which way. THE DOCTOR mumbles something about a
complication. He reaches into her vagina past his
elbow. The pig-faced mother squeals.

                        NURSE
                 (to pig-faced mother)
          Give it some slack. Breathe.
                 (grips pig-faced mother's hand)
          Ok, now. Reel it in! Reel! Reel! Reel!

The doctor pulls out a flapping fish attached by an
umbilical cord. He cuts the cord.

                        DOCTOR
                   (with hand out)
          Blunt instrument.

Nurse hands him a steel pipe. He hits the fish over
the head. The fish convulses and dies.

                                    Back to scene:

UNBLUR to son staring intently at the tip of his
pole. It jerks a few times, then pauses, then doubles
over. He grabs his pole in an excited state.

                         SON
          Mother! I got one!

                          139

                    PIG-FACED MOTHER
          Not too hard. Reel in some line!

The pole bends until it snaps. The son looks at the
broken pole in his hands, then down off the bridge.

                                          Close up on:

A naked body floating face down in the river. It has
stringy red hair spreading out in the water. The
bobber is dragging along behind it.

                         SON
          Mother! There's somebody down there in
          the water.

The son points frantically, drops his broken pole and
runs along the cast-iron railing of the bridge.

                    PIG-FACED MOTHER
          Nonsense!

                         SON
          There it is, it looks dead!

                                            Insert:

Lifeless body floating spread-eagled in the river.

                    PIG-FACED MOTHER
                    (to a passerby)
          Call the police!

She takes off her shoes,[48] climbs up on the rail and
dives into the river, becoming a porkfish when she hits
the water. The son continues along the rail following
his mother's progress along the bank. The porkfish
mother swims gracefully until she catches up with the
body, then nudges it towards shore.

                         SON
          What is it? Is it dead?

                                            Cut to:

Pig-faced mother climbs out, drags the body up on the
meaty bank and feels for a pulse. The body[49] is white

---

[48] Revealing cloven feet.
[49] Of Troy.

as crabmeat and coated in a slimy film. A fleshy growth is hooking from the forehead.

PIG-FACED MOTHER
Run and get some help, son.

The son runs up the stairs cut into the meat cliffs, up to the street level. The pig-faced mother pinches Troy's mouth and listens for air. She is momentarily distracted by the fleshy protrusion, then gets back to the task at hand. She covers Troy's mouth with her lips and blows gently into him. She repeats this, wincing with each effort. After a few cycles it's hard to tell whether she is performing CPR or giving big wet open-mouthed kisses. She is less disgusted with each one. In between breaths she smells and examines his fleshy protrusion.

Close up on:

Milky nectar glistening from the s-cape of his phalangocyte.

Back to scene:

The pig-faced mother kisses him then dabs her pig-tongue on his phalangocyte. She can't resist. She tastes the nectar oozing from the s-cape. She wraps her pig-lips around his entire phalangocyte.

Flash to:

Troy springs to life, gasping wide. He clutches the pig-faced mother and sinks his teeth into her neck. She squeals and flaps around like a fish out of water, but Troy maintains his grip.

Close up on:

Troy's mouth biting into her neck, blood dribbling down, pooling in her suprasternal notch. The pig-faced mother falls limp in his arms.

Troy pulls away and perks his ears. SIRENS are approaching. The sirens stop at the street level just above him.

Cut to:

Son with two paramedics at the top of the stairs.

                              SON
                          (pointing)
           Down there!

                                                        Cut to:

View of meaty riverbank from above. Troy and the pig-
faced mother are both laying side by side on the
bank. From a distance, the pig-faced mother's torso
is in the shape of a boat.

Act V: Scene ii

**The Connection Between Mary X. Lake and the
Containment Pond**

INT. Dream Sequence. Hôpital la Suture, Paris.
November 11, 2005. 1:32 p.m.

It was at this lake where we used to fish for catfish. It was a manmade
lake our father had surveyed.[50] Unlike most of the murky lakes in
Georgia, this lake was clear as a chlorinated swimming pool. A sign
identified it as *Lake Germfree*, though I knew the real name. As a kid,
at this lake, I always wondered what bait looked like to fish when we
were fishing for them and what the fish looked like as they
contemplated the bait. I dove under to find out.

When I opened my eyes I could see perfectly, but saw no fish.
There were hundreds of bare hooks hanging from the surface that I was
careful not to get snagged on.[51] I took off my shorts so they wouldn't
get hooked.[52] I sensed the fish were there but they could see better than
me and were keeping their distance in the open water. The water was
so clear it was black. As I remembered it, there was a shelf near the
shore that John and I suspected was a favorite place for fish to hide.
Taking a deep breath, I went down to look under the shelf. Something
darted in the shadows. I went further under after it. I followed the

---

[50] He noticed it was unnamed so named it after our mother: *Mary X. Lake*.

[51] From my point of view, the surface was a mirror (see footnote 35, replacing
reflection for retaliation). I couldn't tell where the hooks were coming from.

[52] This made sense at the time.

                              142

darting shadow down a passage into complete darkness. Then it got light again and when I emerged I was in the containment pond at the Gaston sewage treatment center. It was night, but the scene was lit by powerful artificial lights. Taking another deep breath, I retreated back to the lake. When I got there, I was in a boat and the lake was now walled in with cliffs of meat.[53] There was a staircase cut into the meat cliff but I was having a hard time paddling toward it as the waves were getting bigger. The meaty shores of the lake were receding. Water splashed on my face that tasted of salt. The salt triggered a premonition of a coming hurricane. I had to decide whether to:

a) go for the stairway cut into the meat cliff or

b) retreat back underwater to the containment pond.

I decided on (b) and hung out with some garbage men who were also there at the artificially lit containment pond waiting the storm out. Their role in this was to pick up garbage in boats to take out to a big barge in the ocean,[54] but they were holding up at the pond because of the storm.[55] One of them asked me[56] if I had called my mother.

[beat]

Then he shouted, "line."

Someone from off the set whispered, "*shouldn't you at least let her know where you're at.*"

The garbage man lawyer repeated this line with more conviction.

When I didn't answer, another of the garbage men lawyers repeated the line again, "shouldn't you at least let her know where you're at?"

I kept brushing it off because I didn't want to come off as a "mommy's boy." All the garbage men lawyers started pitching in, interrogating me like I

---

[53] As in the script.

[54] Or "wide moat," as they called it.

[55] At least that's how things appeared on the surface. I found out later they all had law degrees and were moonlighting as garbage men to "delay execution." When I asked, "execution of what?" they answered, "execution of god's will."

[56] Reading from a script.

was on trial, their voices in unison, sometimes overlapping, over and over, saying, "shouldn't you at least let her know where you're at?[57]"

Act V: Scene iii

Bernard's Inquisition

INT. Dream Sequence. Hôpital la Suture, Paris.
November 11, 2005. 3:13 a.m.

When I showed up[58] for my job interview, my prospective employer[59] took me straight to his private aquarium that was in the adjoining underwater map room.[60] I wasn't sure why he was showing me his aquarium as the newspaper posting listed the position I was applying for as "Continuity Chief for Swamp Survey Crew.[61]" When I asked Bernard if I was in the right place, he told me, "our will that to get." First he wanted to show me his 55-gallon tank that was empty except for five scallops that were evenly spaced at the bottom. There were three black holes in the back wall where fish supposedly lived. "In reality," Bernard said,[62] "live they in a nether tank ay, within a nether tank ay behind a nether wall, beyond a nether, beyond a nether, beyond a nether..." and he kept skipping until I hit him and he stopped, swallowed, and said, "wall. I sashay."

The "wall" was really a movie screen projecting the image of a wall. My mind was reeling trying to figure out what he could possibly be testing me for beyond holistic comprehension. I was on my best behavior, sitting upright and acting interested, ready to field questions, and queuing up questions in my own mind to ask him. But I couldn't

---

[57] I realized I was listening to an old soundtrack on vinyl. The needle wore so deep into the groove it hit a nerve, waking me up.

[58] Fifteen minutes late.

[59] Bernard Verrier.

[60] In the lobby of the Calico Hotel, see dream sequence on page 65.

[61] The description from the *Savannah Mourning News* Want Ads said it was "... for a half land-based half water-based surveying position. As Continuity Chief, you will be responsible for bridging the gap in land/water data."

[62] He was speaking through some sort of scrambling device embedded in his throat.

144

open my mouth.[63] Bernard pulled a lever and five fish darted into the tank and rifled through the scallop shells, stripping them of any meat.[64]

My stomach made a noise and I was sure Bernard noticed, but it didn't show. Once the frenzy was over, the five fish disappeared back into the three holes. I clapped to be polite, and since I couldn't speak. Then he let three snakes into the room. They were writhing at my feet, but I remained calm and courteous. I had to keep reminding myself that I was human and to be myself, but I forgot why I was reminding myself of this.

"Purse severance furthers," he said, pinching the skin on my forearm. "Must they may be able-bodied ay to seize a fold to penetrate, say ye skin. The place of pleasure legitimate ay where they may seize a catch is the strap between ye fingers." I splayed my fingers and he was right—my hands were webbed.[65]

He pinched me again, and then said, "have it known ay that when ye, formally, that I evoke, ay ye do not hatch, in real skin, the contact ay? Our individual skins do not evoke naturally."

I nodded yes, thankful that although there were questions involved, his body language was leading me to the answers. When I looked down at my arm where he had pinched me, a huge chunk had molted off. He didn't notice, or if he did, he did a good job of acting like he didn't.

"Now begins the formulaic segment of the interaction," he said, pressing the record button of a small device. "Do solemnly swear you to tell nothing but the truth?"

JAUNE: [BEAT][66]
BERNARD: Have ye a passport?
JAUNE: [BEAT]
BERNARD: Married are to you?

---

[63] To be more accurate, I could open my mouth, but something was blocking my "voice canal," which at the time was legitimate anatomy.
[64] "Flossing," Bernard called it.
[65] His hands, on the other hand, were not webbed and I was concerned he would judge me for it.
[66] "I do," I thought, but couldn't say.

JAUNE: [BEAT]

BERNARD: Have ye ever, at sea, been on a boat with men, only?

JAUNE: [BEAT]

BERNARD: Ever have ye been an armchair geologist?

JAUNE: [BEAT]

BERNARD: If, hypothetically, you were in effect under assignment to survey a parcel of ground, and looking to the bottom of the map, in the legend, it was your brother... would ye make with the task?

JAUNE: [BEAT][67]

I moved my head in circles and up and down at the same time, until my head rolled off.[68]

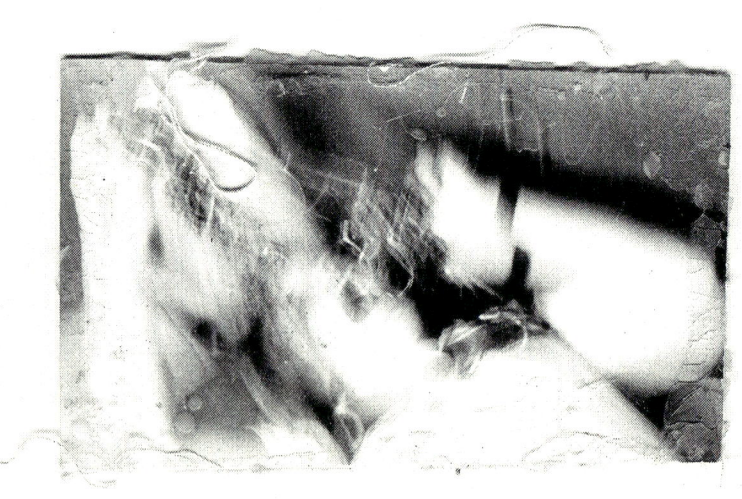

---

[67] Even though I didn't even have the ability to answer the question, the last one threw me for a loop. I never expected to be asked if I would "survey" my own brother, if this in fact was what Bernard was asking, and if in fact John could fit in the legend of the 2-dimensional map.

[68] Waking myself up.

Act V: Scene iv
The Sperm Crawther Plague

INT. Hôpital la Suture, Paris.
November 11, 2005. 10:13 a.m.

I had a third dream[69] about a "crayfish plague." There weren't really any "events" to the dream, except that the plague was brought on by the introduction of an American species of crawdad that wiped out the native variety in France. I wasn't certain where this information came from and could only deduce that I read it while studying for my interview with Bernard.[70]

Marie-Yves came to visit me in the hospital, waking me from deep sleep. I asked her if this was true, in real life, this crayfish plague, and she said "oui." Not only did the fungus itself arrive in the ballast of a ship from America, but in order to combat the plague the French introduced an American species of crayfish called the *Sperm Crawther* that was impervious to the fungus. Since this Sperm Crawther was more resilient than the native French variety, it quickly spread.

"How do you know all this?" I asked Marie-Y.

"Ye are continuity when ye know to need thee abstracts in phylum in order to determine if suspension of disbelief is granted.[71]"

I wake again to Marie-Y knocking on my door. This time it's for real[72] and I pinch myself to be certain. Though one can never be. The boat sculpture is no longer on the wall. I ask Marie-Y if John was here in the room at some point and she says, "Troy?"

"Yes."

"No." When I ask where Troy is she says he, "bar to the left." She opens the blinds, letting light slice up the hospital room.

"He left you at the bar?"

---

[69] Somewhere in between these dreams, John came to visit me. Not Troy, but John. He even admitted to it. As a get-well consolation, he brought me the torso boat sculpture† to hang on the wall here. He thought I might want something "familiar" to liven up the place.

† See page 10.

[70] See previous, *Scene iii: Bernard's Inquisition*.

[71] Marie-Y was speaking through the same brand of scrambler Bernard was speaking through in the previous scene.

[72] For a brief time I mistook her for our mother.

"Yes. That is in fact also.[73]"

She shows me the boils on her skin from worry. "Maybe it should be I the one in here?" She undresses and gets into the hospital bed with me. Unhooking the morphine drip from my arm, she administers it into her vein.

"Just an FYI," I say, "I don't think that's insulin." It's too late. She's hooked in. She pulls the sheet, exposing her webbed feet. I eye her mouth, contemplating. Her lips are thickening into some sort of bill right before my eyes.[74]

I feel flushed. In need of air. I get out of bed, still in gown, wandering the studio grounds searching for Troy. I find him alone, slumped over in the studio bar.[75] There's a tray of uneaten crawdads in front of him.

"I know what you're gonna ask," he says without looking or acknowledging my hospital gown. "There's something you should know first. Something you don't know about yet." He finishes his drink and motions to the bartending actor for another one, and one for me. "Our mother had an abortion."

"How do you know this?"

"She told me. When she was a teenager she had sex with some random guy."

"Where?"

"On a boat. On a lake. She got pregnant from it." Our drinks come.

"That's a weird thing to think about."

"Don't think about it too much then. I just thought you might want to know."

"Did you come see me in the hospital?"

"You know I hate hospitals."

"It's not really a hospital."

"I don't like the idea of them. It crossed my mind to visit though. For your sake."

"Are you going eat those," I ask, motioning to the tray of cold crawdads.

"Have at it."

I pull the crawdads towards me. "We never were into the same habits."

---

[73] From what I could gather from her scrambled story, they were out drinking and she went to the toilet. When she returned he wasn't there. "Before this even, Troy he was not he self." she said. "His direction came from script, not how he would in act his behabits."

[74] Designer collagen implants, fueled by botox.

[75] The set for the French sitcom *Saint Midgets*.

Troy was staring at himself in the mirror behind the bar and jerking his knee up and down. "I feel bad for dragging you all the way out here, and now this, this whole sickness. Are you having any fun?"

"Am I supposed to be?" I say, licking my fingers.

"I hope you're getting something out of it."

"I'm spending quality time with you. And getting to know Marie-Yves." We clink our glasses together.

"I just hope you don't end up like me," says Troy. "This business is a disease. It gets beneath your skin."

The acting bartender brings me an empty plate for the discarded shells then wipes the counter clean in front of us.

Act V: Scene v
Resuscitating Crawdaddy-O

EXT. Banks of the River Seine. Paris.
November 16, 2005. 2:42 p.m.

"Say it like to this you are a newborn!" yells Bernard through his talkie-talkie, gesticulating wildly. "You are a rookie medic. Becoming out of the order! You never saw ever who it was doing the dying. Word he love you to deeply smell it in your heart. Grasp now! That it is perhaps your defect which Troy died."

In the scene, Ron Jeremy[76] and "I" are medics. A boy tells us his mother pulled a body from the river. When we look from the top of the stairs in the meat cliffs, we see two bodies.[77] We descend the stairs with our leather doctor bags and stethoscopes around our necks.

"There is an urgent sense!" yells Bernard.

We run across the pubic hair Astroturf to the bodies. Ron Jeremy takes the pig-faced mother[78] and I get Troy. It's the fifth time we've filmed this scene. I have two lines: "I can't find the vein," and "you're okay." According to Troy, it's enough to get me

---

[76] Evidently Ron Jeremy is a "friend" of Bernard, so he gives him a cameo in every one of his movies.

[77] As noted in the script, from a distance the pig-faced mother is replaced with the torso boat.

[78] Played by Élodée.

into the Screen Actors Guild. I've practiced these two lines until I know them in my sleep.

At first I was a stand-in for the actor playing Medic #1, but the actor that was to play the part got sick, so at the last minute Bernard gave me the part outright. It was only two lines, and being the stand-in I already had them down. "This is it," Troy kept saying before this, "this is your opportunity to break in."

Troy was back in good spirits. Bernard had accepted his phalangocyte cockscomb, and had rewritten the end of the script to accommodate it. Rather than turn into a crawdad, Troy was to morph into a sort of vampire anglerfish with pincers that used his phalangocyte to seduce his victims.[79] Bernard especially liked the sexual connotations of the phalangocyte, and wanted make-up to dress it to simulate a penis. In the insert shot of the pig-faced mother sucking on it, an actual penis was used.[80] And that's when Troy bites her neck and Ron Jeremy and I show up on the scene as medics. Of course Marie-Yves isn't thrilled that Élodée is playing the pig-faced mother, but Bernard insists she is perfect for the part.[81]

Being that Troy had morphed into a half-angler-half-cray fish and wasn't able to "run" away, he figures his best option is to play dead. This is what the anglerfish in him is best at doing. Since we are fresh on the scene, we have no idea what happened and assume it is some sort of homicide gone bad.

"You cannot with confidence trust what says the son to you!" yells Bernard. "That it snagged a fish of Troy and our mother pig drew out of the river. You must suppose the boy is in the shock to see his matrix of mother rise before his eyes. You cannot comfort it now because your hands are not complete!"

Ron Jeremy is administering to the pig-faced mother, while I'm trying to resuscitate Troy. Ron throws in a line not from the script: "textbook shock. Slap her around, she'll come to."

I'm not comfortable improvising. I watch as my body pulls a shot of epinephrine from my bag and that's when "I" speak my first real line: "I can't find the vein.[82]"

---

[79] The title of the film was even changed accordingly to *The Vampire Angler and the Heroine Heir to Notre Dame.*

[80] Albeit flaccid. And the head was never truly exposed.

[81] Marie-Y claims Élodée "blew on Bernard" for the part.

[82] In my mind I'm a rookie medic that has never seen action so I'm supposed to be freaked out by it all. In reality, I *am* freaked out about it, being my first acting role, and on top of it all, seeing my brother in this condition, even if it's not real.

In an earlier version of the script, Bernard had Medic #1 seduced by Troy's phalangocyte, but I said no way. That was taking it too far. And it was really an inconsequential act, a "last request," as Bernard called it, before Troy vanished into the river in a cloud of "galactic dust and jumping porkfishes." It's hard enough administering CPR on Troy knowing he's my brother. He's made up to be a vampire angler-crayfish, but underneath it all I know who Troy is.[83] At least in rehearsal and the first few botched takes I did. Bernard kept cutting me off, yelling, telling me I needed to stop "acting to act," and say it from my heart. And here we are.

It's just one line — I can't find the vein — that I need to say. Marie-Y coaches me to say it with conviction. The angler-crayfish, ex-Crawdaddy-O, has collapsed veins so there is nowhere to get the needle in.[84] Not a good first patient for a rookie medic. Ron Jeremy has already ripped open Élodée's shirt and is pounding on her exposed chest trying to resuscitate her. He is the veteran medic, giving me advice for my patient while trying to bring the pig-faced mother back to life.

"Classic junkie," he says, diverting from the script again. "We see these every day. Though I've never seen one with a cock on his forehead." He advises me to look for a vein in his neck. As this goes on, I realize Bernard has not yelled cut, that this is the take. This is the money shot. As I'm searching for a vein in his neck, Troy whispers to me out of the corner of his mouth. I expect him to tell me, as scripted, that he, "needs a boat," but what I hear is he needs to go back to the water.[85] He's a fish. He needs the river. "Release me," he says repeatedly. His acting is so good I'm not aware it's Troy. I'm not aware he is my brother. He is a character I have created in my mind.[86] That's when I say my other line, "you're okay," though I wished I had been given something else.

Crawdaddy-O comes to life, wiggling the tip of his tail. Then, in characteristic crawdad fashion, he curl-thrusts his tail, and disappears into a cloud of "galactic dust." We hear a splash in the river and see porkfishes jumping in his wake.[87] When the dust settles, Crawdaddy-O is gone. The camera keeps rolling as the

---

[83] Or rather, John.

[84] This is my motive.

[85] When I ask after why he didn't stick to his lines, he said they didn't make sense in the moment.

[86] Projected onto Troy, onto Œuf and Egg, onto Oph, and onto John.

[87] To be edited in after the fact.

151

ripples ebb. Bernard whispers, "the indivisible effects of the divisible effects manifest themselves and ... cut!" Everyone on the crew erupts in applause.[88]

Savannah Mourning News—April 30, 2006

Oph White Dethroned: *Crawdaddy-O & The Heroine Heir to Notre Dame*

In this latest head-scratching escapade from Savannah's own Oph White (formerly know as John White), White has further distanced himself from our Savannah, not only with a superficial name change, but by teaming up with the late French director Bernard Verrier, in the B-grade production of *Crawdaddy-O & the Heroine Heir to Notre Dame*.

The roles that White has chosen have become increasingly bizarre, thusly I braced myself for the worst as this indulgent sci-fi thriller unfolded, splintered, reformed, folded back on itself, fractured, and eventually imploded on itself. White plays Troy, a somnambulist junkie screenwriter who sets off for Paris to work on a script. That is about the extent of what I could glean from the film,

shot entirely on location in France. From there, Troy's identity is transcendental and reality is approximate. His character transforms into some sort of crayfish, Crawdaddy-O, that by the end becomes more of an anglerfish. Certainly, it's a curio that will provoke and be controversial, as intended, but you'll be left wondering what the hell you just sat through.

Despite shooting the film in English, Verrier (who died of an apparent heroin overdose towards the end of the movie) has further alienated the American audience, an audience that was already hemorrhaging after his bomb *Pinocchio & the Arthropodal Héroïne* (a sort of prequel to *Crawdaddy-O & the Heroine Heir to Notre Dame*)

---

[88] It was the first time I'd heard people on the crew applaud a take while we were filming it.

In this sequel, Pinocchio is demoted (or promoted, depending on the way you look at it) to being the bad guy, perhaps indicative of Verrier's true relationship with the actor that plays Pinocchio, Big Bubba Dixon (locals might be interested to know that the stand-in for Big Bubba Dixon, Jamil Crawford, originally hails from Beaufort, SC). Bernard Verrier has been known for using the lead roles in his film to entice would-be lovers (male or female). Rumors abounded before filming started about the nature of the relationship between White and Verrier, but the word on the set was that White was dating continuity, Marie-Yves Curie (though other sources say that towards the end of the film he was seen frequently with Élodée Rouge, the assistant to the make-up artist).

After a series of misadventures, the protagonist Troy visits the Porkfish Belly Bar, where he first meets Pinocchio and his introduction to "bug juice," a narcotic that makes your perceive the grotesque arthropodal nature of others, as well as yourself. The shoddy production values do nothing to help you buy into this absurd story, that cascades into absurd non sequiturs and head-scratching biological metaphors that appear to only make sense to Verrier's perverse imagination. Despite the incomprehensibility, an apparent rift develops midway through the movie that seems more indicative of the goings-on on the set, than what is scripted, perhaps coinciding with the events leading up to the death (in real life) of Bernard Verrier. Hardly a

coincidence, as co-directorial duties of the film were assumed by White and Curie following Verrier's death. White's role shifts from being the hero Crawdaddy-O to being an anglerfish traitor, a dead one at that. (There, I gave it away without remorse. I did this because it is really not recommended you see this movie, unless you are curious as to what has become of our John White.)

Perhaps at the end we can call him an anti-hero. After this series of misadventures, the anglerfish incarnation of Troy ends up on the banks of the river Seine, operated on by a medic, who strangely enough is also played by White. (Also of interest is that the other medic is played by the porn star Ron Jeremy). The fate of Crawdaddy-O is in the hands of the medic, or himself!

At first, the abrupt shift and premature "death" of Troy/ Crawdaddy-O/Anglerfish, not to mention the frequent allusions of the film to itself and the making of it, made this viewer wonder how much of the movie was un-scripted and improvised, spurned by drama on the set?

In it's finer moments, this is a movie about transformation, redemption and second-chances. When the surreal fog clears (when he is pulled from the river for a second time), The Anglerfish returns, not as Troy, but as "Yolk," altogether a different character, but nevertheless still the protagonist. The snow falling and melting on the new and revitalized face of Troy brings to mind the scene in *Wizard of Oz* where Dorothy wakes up in the poppy fields. Troy is no

153

longer Crawdaddy-O or an Anglerfish, but for the rest of the movie he is accompanied by a crawdad, a marsupial newt, some sort of boat manikin and a platypus that he keeps in his satchel, a blatant and surreal amalgamation of *Oz* and *Beastmaster*, made even stranger in that the marsupial newt, his girlfriend, also keeps him as a "fetish" in her own pouch, leading to spiraling bouts of illogic that I would challenge even David Lynch to make sense of. As in *Oz*, all four characters (existing really in the head of Yolk), all seek their mother, the anglerfish (cloned from Crawdaddy-O), but for different reasons. The inclusion of flashbacks to his childhood, while of interest to locals as they allude to the swampy backwoods of Georgia (one scene even has recreated tombs from Bonaventure cemetery), make me wonder if they were Oph's own indulgent doing. And towards the end we discover that the whole story takes place in the mind of Yolk!? Troy ends up the belly of a whale, a blatant rip-off of Pinocchio.

What's initially involving becomes self-involved. Interest languishes and meaning disappears as the plot disappears up its own tortuous "tubiforms". In the end Crawdaddy-O is buried. But we are still unsure whether he died. After a year, they unearth the casket and no body is found. No body, no murder. Not even a trace of DNA. The "Schrödinger's Cat" defense is used in the trial, which digresses into a lecture on quantum mechanics and it's implications on forensic evidence.

If this all sounds pretentious and over-the-top, it's because it is. I'd question whether Oph White even knows what the film is about, or whether he understood Bernard's original vision. I'd go further to say that beyond plain bad, this movie is dangerous. There is nothing to be redeemed from it. It is the product of a sick and lost mind, whose head has been up his own ass ever since he left Savannah.

Act V: Scene vi
The Subtextual Firing of Troy

INT. Notre Dame. Paris.
November 16, 2005. 2:42 p.m.

Everything was going along just fine.[89] That's usually how it happens. We had just finished the scene where Troy steals a line from Jiminy Cricket.[90] We were all shooting the shit, occasionally sniffing each other up. Troy and Bernard were even getting along.[91] Ron Jeremy was admiring Troy's "forehead cock," as he called it. Bernard said it "appears as the red thing on a cock's head.[92]" He asked Troy if he could "finger" it and without waiting for an answer he reached out with his finger cocked to flick. The instant he made contact, Troy snapped forward and locked onto Bernard's wrist.[93,94] When Bernard got back to his feet, he fired Troy.[95]

---

[89] We were all standing around inside the artificially lit Notre Dame (the real thing, not a studio) eating tuna and crackers and drinking wine from the Kraft table. The cathedral was closed to the public while we were shooting the scene where Crawdaddy-O crawls down the aisle and begs for penance at the altar. Troy was dressed as Crawdaddy-O. I was back to being his stand-in so was dressed as a half-ass Crawdaddy-O, in a red suit of the same proportions. Élodée was hanging on Troy's shoulder, under the pretense of removing his make-up. Marie-Yves didn't even care that Élodée was all over him (or at least she was acting like she didn't). Marie-Y was acquiring a legion of suitors of her own—shy, green-headed extras hired to flesh out the pews (though they had their own *raisons d'être*). Marie-Y's forming duckbill lips (real collagen implants, fueled by botox) were a coveted feature to these green-headed Frenchmen (though they were too busy squabbling with each other to do anything tangible about it).

[90] *What does an actor want with a conscience anyway?*

[91] At least they were acting like it. Everyone acted, especially when they weren't officially acting.

[92] I tried to inform him that "cockscomb" was the word he was thinking of, but my talkie-talkie wouldn't translate it to French.

[93] Bernard tried to bite back, but Troy went into a rage pummeling Bernard with his faux plush claws. They went tumbling into the pews, with Troy on top, yelling, "I'm not your puppet," with each hit. We were all too engrossed to do anything about it. You couldn't script it any better. Finally, one of the gaffers loyal to Bernard pulled Troy off.

[94] Marie-Y had the presence of mind to roll the camera.

[95] Troy threw off his Crawdaddy-O mitts and stormed down the aisle of Notre Dame. I picked up the faux claws and asked Marie-Y what to do with them. The camera was still rolling. She panned over to me.

155

Act VI: Scene i
Getting It Past the Maître D'

EXT. Night. Ave Champs Elysées, Paris.
November 21, 2005.

                                        Flash on:

Troy maniacally driving a flesh-colored Nandi. Marie-
Yves in the passenger seat. Jaune is sleeping in
back.

                    MARIE-YVES
        You have not to drive like a crazy!

                      TROY
        It's not me, it's your car. Listen to
        that, the clutch is all fucked up. I
        can't downshift. We just need to keep
        going.

To get around another car, Troy drives up on the
sidewalk, sideswiping a parking meter and knocking
the side mirror clean off. Some PEDESTRIANS jump out
of the way as Troy honks his horn. He runs over a
trashcan that gets wedged under the Nandi before
lurching back on the road.

Marie-Y punches in the dashboard lighter and wedges a
cigarette between her duck-billed lips.

                      TROY
        Don't stress. We'll expense it.

                                        Cut to:

Jaune waking up amidst swirling cigarette smoke. He
stares out the back window. He nonchalantly fingers
the skin near his wrist, peeling pieces off.

                                        Cut to:

Troy looking into the rearview mirror. He is
distracted by the phalangocyte dangling off his
forehead. He eyes it with crossed eyes.

                        156

                    MARIE-YVES
        Why do you have such hurry? Kill us you
        will before we arrive.

                       TROY
        You're right. There is no hurry. After
        all, I'm dead now. I've been written out
        of the script. I have nowhere to go.

                    MARIE-YVES
        It is not you to have such drama.
        Bernard no can write you out of the
        script not with such ease. There are
        remains scenes for to finish.

                       TROY
        The only shots left are of Crawdaddy-O
        dead. Anybody that can swim and stand
        wearing that plush suit can play that
        part.

                                           Cut to:

Façade and sidewalk in front of the Restaurant Beger.

                       TROY
        What the fuck, no valet parking?

Troy drives the Nandi up on the sidewalk to the shock
of TWO COUPLES smoking outside the restaurant.

                       TROY
        Let them tow it. Bernard will foot the
        bill.

Troy gets out, doesn't even shut his door. Jaune gets
out on the same side but doesn't shut the door.
Marie-Y goes around to shut it for them.

                                         Flash on:

Pile of dogshit.

                                           Cut to:

Jaune sidestepping the dogshit. As Troy approaches
the restaurant, the MAÎTRE D' holds up his hand to
stop him. He says something in French.

                       TROY
        What's this all about?
                       157

                    MARIE-YVES
          He likes not the style in which you
          dress.

Troy is wearing green leather motorcycle pants, flip-
flops with "Malibu" embroidered on them and a mustard
colored felt jacket. His phalangocyte cockscomb
protrudes from his forehead.

Marie-Y is wearing a puffy yak fur coat and snakeskin
pants. By this time, her botoxed lips are fully
formed into a duckbill.

Jaune is wearing a white monkey suit with his name
embroidered on it.

                      TROY
          I don't particularly like the way he is
          dressed either. Does he know who I am?

                    MARIE-YVES
          This is sucks. We go to this every
          time. It matters not who you are. It is
          your attitude that keeps us from
          gaining entrance to a place.

                      TROY
             (holding up the collar of his jacket)
          Tres chic a la mode. This is a vintage
          Austrian hunting jacket. It cost me
          beaucoup stitches.

A COUPLE brushes by them and the guy hands the maître
d' a 10-euro note. The maître d' sniffs their armpits
and rubs against them as he lets them pass.

                      TROY
             (pulling out a wad of bills)
          So that's how it is.

Troy stuffs a 100-stitch bill into the maître d's
coat pocket. The maître d' is unphased.

                    MARIE-YVES
          Are you an idiot? Studio money is here
          not exchanged.

Marie-Y pulls out a 20-euro note and hands it to the
maître d'. The maître d' sniffs Marie-Y's armpits,
rubs against her, presumably compliments her on her

duckbill and lets her pass. He eyes Troy's
phalangocyte with suspicion and disgust, but
reluctantly lets him enter. He doesn't even notice
Jaune.

Act VI: Scene ii
Ruminant Correction

INT. Night. White's Residence, Savannah, GA
January 13, 2006.

Craw (krô) n.

The pouch-like sac or gullet of an insect's digestive tract in which food
is partially digested or stored for regurgitating to offspring. *Of unknown
origin.*

159

Act VI: Scene iii
Table for Two

INT. Night. Restaurant Beger, Paris.
November 21, 2005.

Marie-Yves is seated between Jaune and Troy in a
restaurant booth upholstered with red and orange
striped pleather.

> JAUNE
> That was a waste of one hundred
> stitches.

> TROY
> Garçon!

> JAUNE
> Then again, what are you going to do
> with your stitches when you get back to
> the states?

Marie-Y holds her hand in the air and signals to a
WAITER. The waiter approaches, throws two menus on
the table and walks away.

> JAUNE
> What's wrong with these people? Can't
> they see there's three of us?

> MARIE-YVES
> *(rolling her eyes)*
> Not can you two comprehend the menu
> regardless. People come to here for one
> reason only and this is for fondue.

The waiter comes back with two table settings and two
glasses of water.

> TROY
> Garçon, can we get some wine here?

The waiter walks away without a word.

> TROY
> Hello?!

                    MARIE-YVES
        He sees you. It is by His choice he
        disregards you.
                    (puts down her napkin)
        Excuse of me. You can let me go to do
        my toilet.

                                        Cut to:

Marie-Yves sliding out of the booth and Troy sitting
back down.

                    MARIE-YVES
        And no you leave me when I'm away.

Act VI: Scene iv
On the Mating Rituals of *Astacus Disgenes*

INT. TV White's Residence, Savannah, GA
January 14, 2006.

[in the voice of Richard Attenborough]
". . . While the female is molting, the male crawdad flips her supine.
They are the only other species besides humans that are known to do it
missionary style. Once the sperm is implanted, the regeneration of the
shell begins. It is at this critical stage of development that the female of
the species is most vulnerable to outside predation. Once impregnated,
the male digs a burrow for the female and puts her inside. Then he
stands guard outside, leaving only to forage for food to feed the female.
He keeps this up for two weeks until her shell has grown back and the
female can leave the burrow . . ."

Act VI: Scene v
Spawn Role Reversal

INT. Night. Restaurant Beger, Paris.
November 21, 2005.

                                        Flash on:

Marie-Yves disappearing behind a door that says W.C.

                                        Cut to:

Jaune sitting with Troy.

                    JAUNE
        What was that all about it?

                    TROY
        She has serious abandonment issues.

                                    Close up on:

Troy, staring at his phalangocyte cockscomb with
crossed eyes. He impulsively lunges for it, his lower
jaw jutting, but of course he misses. He watches with
jaw jerking as the phalangocyte pendulums back and
forth in front of his eyes.

                    JAUNE
        She told me about the incident in the
        bar. Where you abandoned her.

                    TROY
        It was an accident, not an incident.

                    JAUNE
        How could you forget her like that?

                    TROY
        You want to try being me?

Troy lunges at his phalangocyte and actually gets a
hold of it. He rips it out leaving a hole in his
forehead oozing with blood. He hands it to Jaune.
Jaune examines the severed phalangocyte.

                    JAUNE
        I don't want your ... whatever it is.

                         TROY
              (licks base of the phalangocyte,
              presses it to Jaune's forehead)
         There. I anoint you as me. Now you can
         have Marie-Y all to yourself.

                         JAUNE
         What's that supposed to mean?

The phalangocyte sticks. Troy dabs the hole left in
his forehead with a cloth napkin.
                                              Cut to:

Marie-Y examining her duckbill in the bathroom mirror
as she applies make-up. She looks more like a porkfish
than a duck. She is not used to putting make-up on her
proboscis bill. She botches on some red lipstick,
purses her bill-lips together and exits the bathroom.

                                              Cut to:

Troy getting up to let Marie-Y slide back into the booth
between him and Jaune, who now wears the phalangocyte.

                         JAUNE
         Aren't you hot in that thing?

Marie-Y takes off her yak-fur coat. She is wearing
nothing but snakeskin pants underneath.

                         TROY
         Any particular reason you're shirtless?

                       MARIE-YVES
         My nipples hurt. See how hard they is?

                         TROY
         I'm sure the botox treatment doesn't help.

                       MARIE-YVES
         This not has to do about it. I am how
         do you say, with a child in my belly.

                         JAUNE
         Pregnant?

                         TROY
         You don't look it.

                       MARIE-YVES
         Believe me when I say I am.
                          163

Act VI: Scene vi
Salamandrine Alias

EXT. Day. Intracoastal waterway, GA.
March 29, 1971.

Hand over hand, I draw the wet cord. I pretend I'm lifting the anchor to something. The shore we stand on is unsteady. When it gets close, John lifts the cage out of the water. Sopping algae drips off the chicken-wire mesh. Spanish moss drips from the oak branches over our heads. The din of cicadas is deafening.

"What the hell is that?" I ask.

"Ain't no crawdad, that's for sure," says John.

"It's a mamnewt."

"I don't think so. Salamander is more like it."

"Same difference."

"Salamanders have external gills." John points to a bronchial appendage coming off the side of the salamander's cheek. "I saw it in a book once."

"Look," I say. "It's forming a bill. And its skin is more like fur."

"It's some sort of platypus salamander. I've read about these too."

"What keeps fish from chewing off these phalangey gills? If I was a fish I'd sure like to eat those."

"You would," says John.

"Looks like chewed up worms." I finger at the external gills. They are rubbery and slimy. I muster the courage to stroke the fur.

"It's poisonous," says John. "See the orange underbelly? That's a dead giveaway."

I withdraw my hand. "Is it dead or playing dead?"

"Drowned probably. It's an amphibian. It needs air sometimes. The trap trapped it underwater." John opens it up and lets the dead mamnewt out.

"We didn't catch a single crawdad."

"The salamander must have scared 'em off." John picks the mamnewt up by the tail and throws it back into the paludal water. It sinks for a second, then floats belly up on the surface.

"Isn't she a keeper?"

"Not even." John flips the can-opener blade from his pocketknife and pries two jagged slots in a new can of tuna. Opens the latch of the cage and reaches in. Takes the old can out and flips it into the river. "Chum," he says.

He wires the new can to the bottom of the cage then closes it up. The label on the can says ICF for Intra-Coastal Fisheries. John stands up, shuts his pocketknife and slips it in his front pocket. Wipes his hands on his already muddied pants.

I pick up the cage to cast it back out but John takes it from me. "We have to get it out far into the deep part this time," he says, coiling back to throw.

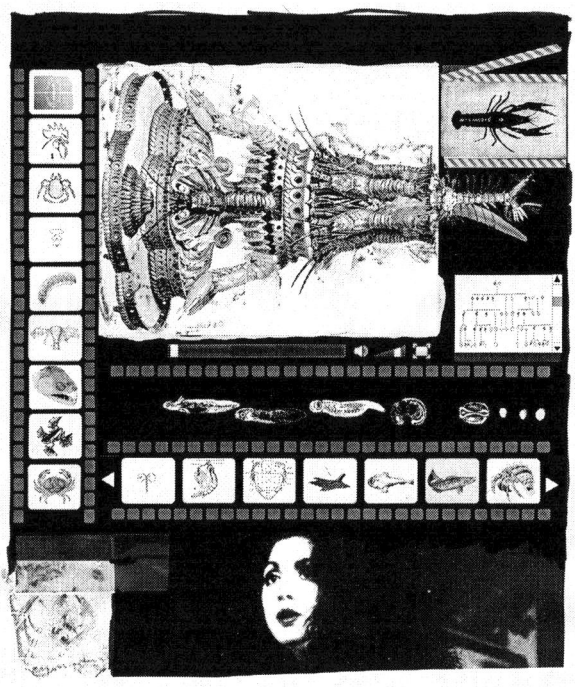

165

Act VI: Scene vii
Marie-Yves Rejects the First Take

INT. Night. Restaurant Beger, Paris.
November 21, 2005.

                                              Cut to:

Jaune, with disturbed look on his face.

                          JAUNE
           It smells disgusting. Are we sure we
           want to eat here?

                        MARIE-YVES
                    (lighting a cigarette,
                     noticeably irritated)
           After all these problems to gain
           entrance? You are lucky for here to be.
                    (exhales a cloud of smoke)
           This is the cheese you smell.

Marie-Y signals to the waiter. He comes to the table.
If he notices she is topless it doesn't show on his
face.

                        MARIE-YVES
           Un bouteille du vin et un fondue de
           Fromage pour deux.

The waiter nods, sniffs his way up her outstretched
arm to her hairy pit, then returns to the kitchen.

                          TROY
           Do you think it's such a good idea to
           be smoking now that you're pregnant?

Marie-Y exhales. Takes another drag. The waiter
returns with a bottle of wine and two glasses.

                          TROY
                    (waving three fingers in the
                     waiter's face)
           Bonjour! We are three here.

The waiter, oblivious to Troy, pours a glass for
Marie-Y. She tries it, spits it on the floor and
sends it back with a wave of her hand.

                          166

Act VI: Scene viii
On the Sense of Smell of *Procamburus Nubbsi*

INT. TV, Night. White's Residence, Savannah, GA
January 14, 2006.

[in the voice of Richard Attenborough]
". . . the crawdad's sense of smell is one of the most acute of any biological creature. Compared to humans, it is ten thousand times more sensitive. It is impossible for us to imagine the information crawdads can extract from smell. They render a picture of the world through olfactory sensations akin to us seeing in color. In the murky medium that crawdads live, visibility is poor. Smells are held in suspension by the water, and are able to travel around corners and into the nooks and crannies where crawdads dwell. From this soup of olfactory information, crawdads can render a map of their worlds . . ."

Act VI: Scene ix
Takes Two and Three

INT. Night. Restaurant Beger, Paris.
November 21, 2005.

                                                    Cut to:

Waiter returning to the kitchen with the bottle of opened wine.

                    MARIE-YVES
        This is sucks! They think that for why
        I'm with Americans they can pass wine
        corked off on to me.

                    TROY
        You don't need to say, "this *is* sucks,"
        just, "this sucks."

                    MARIE-YVES
          As of when are you a police with my
          English? For less I try.

They sit in silence. Jaune periodically lunges at his
newfound phalangocyte. Troy shakes up a bottle of
olive oil on the table and stares at the spices and
long strands of rosemary in suspension.

                                            Cut to:

The waiter brings out a second bottle of wine and
opens it there at the table. He takes the cork and
rubs it on Marie-Y's porkfish bill lips.

                      TROY
              (punching Jaune on the arm)
          Are you seeing this shit? This guy's
          got a lot of nerve.

Marie-Y tries the wine and spits it back into the
glass. Sends it back with a wave of her hand.

                      TROY
          Maybe you could get him to bring out
          some bread while you're at it.
          Something substantial.

                                            Cut to:

The waiter brings out a third bottle and opens it.
Marie-Yves tries it, winces in distaste but accepts
it with a resigned nod. The waiter fills two glasses.

                      TROY
          Hey, un *otre* glass *si vous plait*! And
          don't forget bread. We want *pain*.

Troy motions to his open mouth with bunched up
fingertips. The waiter looks right in his direction
with an expressionless face then turns away.

                    MARIE-YVES
          Even this wine is not so good. But I am
          sucks off this. This is *merde*.

                      TROY
          I wouldn't know. I don't even have a
          glass.

                        168

                    MARIE-YVES
          (sighs, lights another cigarette)
     Can we stop this, this role-playing?
     For one night? Can you for less decide
     who you want to be?

They sit in silence, Jaune tapping his glass with his
fork, tapping to validate its existence, to keep the
focus off his dangling phalangocyte.

[BEAT]

Troy picks up the bottle of wine with two hands and
drinks straight from it. He polishes off the bottle
in three tries. Reaches for Jaune's glass and
finishes it off too. Holds the empty glass up to his
ear. Marie-Y finishes her own.

                      TROY
               (noticeably drunk,
             still holding glass to ear)
     I remember once we were out at Tybee
     Island and I found one of those big
     conch shells, the big swirly ones with
     the pink insides. I showed it to our
     mother and she held it up to my ear and
     told me the sea was inside. For the
     longest time I fell for it. What a sap
     I was. Now I know better. If you put
     your mind to it, you can hear the sea
     in just about any cavity.

                     JAUNE
          (holds up his empty glass)
     Let's make a toast. Here's to our
     mother.

                      TROY
     Forget about our fucking mother.

                     JAUNE
     Okay, here's to Troy.

                      TROY
          (holds up his imaginary glass)
     Here's to the death of Troy.

                  MARIE-YVES
     Attention! This is not good luck to
     make health with empty vessels. We need
     more wine first.

Act VII: Scene i
The Truth About Troy

EXT. Day. Troy.
Circa 12th century B.C.

"The body of Paris is returned to his father and the Iliad ends with the funeral rites of the Trojan hero," says John.

"Is that it?"

"What do you mean is that it? 'It' lasted ten years. A ten-year battle, all fought over Helen of Troy."

"She must have been something."

John builds up a pile of twigs and sets Paris on top of it. Squirts some lighter fluid all over it and lets it soak in. Then he lights the funeral pyre. The crawdad sinks into the twigs as they catch fire. It struggles a bit and cooks, giving off a hissing sound. The smoke rises up into the boughs of the sweet gums and magnolia trees, filtering through the Spanish moss.

"You're going to hell for this," I say.

"Only if you think so."

"What about the horse?"

"What horse?"

"That wooden horse they used to get into the Trojan compound. That's what I think of."

"The war continued thereafter. Achilles was eventually slain. Many of the heroes died and finally—making use of the famous trick of the horse—the Achaean forces managed to penetrate Troy. The city was destroyed and looted, Helen was returned to Menelaus, and the victorious army sailed for home. But that's not what's important here."

John scoops up the burning crawdad who we dubbed as Paris and sets him on a piece of bark. We roll up our pant legs and wade in up to our knees. John sets him asail into the slow moving and murky Savannah River. The burning pyre drifts out to sea with the outgoing tide.

"This story ends with the death of Paris," says John. "He becomes one with the sea."

Act VII: Scene ii
On the Sex Life of the Trojan Bluegill

INT. TV, Night. White's Residence, Savannah, GA
January 14, 2006.

[in the voice of Richard Attenborough]
". . . while transsexualty in humans does not put them at a reproductive advantage, this is not the case with transsexual Trojan bluegills. These fish have developed a cunning way to propagate their seed in an otherwise alpha-male dominated pond. Most Trojan bluegill males are considerably larger than the females. They typically have harems of smaller females to which they claim reproductive bragging rights.

At some point during a male juvenile's development, he decides whether he wants to compete with the large alpha-males or opt for a sneakier route. Rather than grow large, these transsexual males grow to the same size as females and are virtually indistinguishable. Mistaking them for females, the alpha-male courts them into his harem and even provides them with protection. When the females are ready to mate, the transsexual males are first in line. They are able to sneak in and impregnate them while the alpha male is busy fending off intruders . . ."

Act VII: Scene iii
Our Scaly Scent

INT. Night. Orly International, Paris.
November 22, 2005.

"I'm sorry with feeling who have to sit on the plane beside Troy," says Marie-Yves. "We do smell so." She drapes her arms around my neck and rests her head on my shoulder, looking off in the direction Troy disappeared to. She doesn't care that my skin is raw and red and oozing with pus. She's accepted my molting. I'm prepared to blame it on Troy if she asks. Normally I'm sensitive to the touch, but I don't mind Marie-Y's. She feels cold and clammy.

"Yes," I say. "We really reek."

It's been almost a full day and we still smell of the cheese fondue. Troy has boarded his plane and Marie-Y and I are left standing in the terminal. All three of us share this smell. When we were all three together it wasn't so bad. It was bonding in a sense. Now Troy is alone in smelling up his plane that is taxiing down the runway. His final words were, in the voice of Brody, "we're gonna need a bigger boat." When I asked what he meant by it, he only added, "as in ark. Like Noah." Marie-Y did not cry when Troy boarded his plane but now she looks like she might.

"There is a part of me going to miss him," she says. "Even if I do like this way feels better. Troy was a mean to me. I was another grouper for him," she says.

There's no option except to hug her back. "I think you mean 'groupie'," I say. "Not grouper. Grouper's a kind of fish."

Marie-Y wipes her eyes and says she needs a drink. She unwraps her arms from around my neck. I'm self-conscious of the scales of her left on me. The evidence is mounting.

Act VII: Scene iv
Defining the Mamnewt

INT. Night. White's Residence, Savannah, GA
January 23, 2006.

Mamnewt (mamnyüt):

1. A salamander of genus *triturus* living chiefly on land but aquatic during breeding season. Mamnewts also contain a marsupial pouch unlike their salamander sisters.

Salamander (sál-e-man-der):

1. Any of various small lizard-like amphibians of the order *Caudata*, having porous scaleless skin and four, often weak or rudimentary legs.

2. An object, such as a poker, used in a fire.

3. A mythical creature capable of living in or withstanding fire.

Act VII: Scene v
Down the Platypus Fire Pole

INT. Lili Le Tigrese Bar, Paris.
November 23, 2004. 12:50 a.m.

As we enter the bar, Marie-Yves sees Thierry, the chain-smoking gaffer. "Don't you to worry," she says, waving toward him. "Just for a temporary piece of fun."

"Let's don't call him over," I say. "That guy drives Jaune nuts."

It was too late. Thierry saw her and made his way through the crowd. He had a girl in tow that I hadn't seen on the set.

"¿Ce va?"

"Ce va."

Routine armpit smelling and rubdowns. Thierry introduces the girl he is with as Lauren or Lorraine—I can't really make out her name with the music. "This is Marie-Yves and Troy."

I smell perfume emanating from her armpits.

"Troy?" she repeats back as she rubs herself against me.

"Actually, my name is Jaune."

Thierry rolls his eyes. "No can I stay up with you ever, always changing your name." He eyes Jaune's phalangocyte cockscomb dangling from my forehead. "I thought it was Troy the one with the annexe. Now you have acquired one?"

"Ooooh," says Lauren. "Super cool. I have been told of these and here is one." She rubs it between her two fingers. Jaune's mouth lunges at her hand before I stop him.

"Sorry," I say. "Jaune is new to this. He needs to learn self-restraint."

"This is okay," she says, placing her hand on Jaune's crotch.

I look to Marie-Y for assistance. "Don't worry," Marie-Y says. "This is acceptable. We are in a bar. She is becoming family to you."

It's hard to talk with all the noise in the bar let alone the hand on my crotch. I watch as a topless dancer comes swirling down a fire pole onto the counter. We tried to go to this bar before with Troy, but of course they wouldn't let him in on account of his attitude. Marie-Y and Thierry are carrying on in French. Lauren loses interest in palming Jaune's crotch. Marie-Y grabs at Jaune's arm, laughing, "Thierry says he smells a cheese."

She continues laughing and talking in French with Thierry and Lauren.

"What are you guys talking about?" Jaune asks.

"Your scene with the pornography hero," says Marie-Y. "In where you try to save your brother."

"*I can't find the vein*," says Thierry, imitating Jaune's acting.

"We were saying it is good for you to consume oranges," says Lauren. "And to go for long walks." She is easier to understand than Marie-Y.

"Why?" Jaune asks. My skin is getting flushed. I want to take off the itchy sweater Jaune is wearing, but the skin on my arms is all raw and chaffed beneath it and I'm afraid of smelling even worse.

"To clean inside-out your glands and pores. Marie-Y tells me you ate fondue at Restaurant Beger last night?"

"Oh yes, that."

Then I see Élodée across the room. She is still made up as the pig-faced mother. She makes her way over to us. At first she eyes only the phalangocyte, her face glowing to see it. Then her eyes shift down and she realizes Jaune is not Troy. She still sniffs Jaune's armpits. "Ou est Troy?" she asks while rubbing against me. "What occurred to him?"

"Troy went back to America," Jaune says.

"And not for you to think once about stealing his brother," says Marie-Y. "Troy left him for me." Marie-Y throws her arms around Jaune's neck and hangs on. I get a waft of the cheese smell and don't know if it's Jaune or her. The stench is starting to make me nauseous. Élodée lingers, as if to consider challenging Marie-Y, cringes her pig-nose, then spins around and leaves. Marie-Y places her cigarette in her duckbill lips to free up her hands to clap. The cigarette is dangling precariously close to Jaune's ear.

"Watch it!" I say. "You're going to burn Jaune with that!"

"Her look you like?" asks Marie-Y.

"Jaune likes you as platy-pussy," I say.

Marie-Y reaches into her purse. "I am near to forget." She jabs a syringe into a vial and injects herself with botox. Applies lipstick to her bill. Another dancer swirls down the fire pole. Thierry says something to Marie-Yves and she starts laughing.

"What's so funny?" Jaune asks.

"Thierry is saying that, how do you say, for the price of one I got two."

"You're drunk."

174

"I am not so," Marie-Yves says, disengaging Jaune from her grasp. She sips her Margarita through her swollen porkfish lips.

Jaune rubs my stinging eyes. Everybody gets quiet all of a sudden.

"We were in a joke," says Thierry. "We are so happy for to see Troy gone and Yuck in."

"Yolk," Jaune says.

They all laugh then joke around in French. Jaune's skin is burning me. During Troy's time I was comfortable feeling uncomfortable, it was part of who I was, but now as Jaune I'm truly uncomfortable and having a hard time veiling it.

"Are you okay with this all?" asks Marie-Y with genuine concern.

"Yes," Jaune says. "This is fun. Jaune likes this bar very much."

"You are not tired? Your eyes are red."

"It's just the smoke. And it's hot and stuffy in here." Truth is I'm swelling and overheating. The shell of Jaune is combusting me. Everyone in the bar can probably smell both Marie-Y and I. All I can think about is a cold shower and my brother. Jaune struggles to understand what Thierry is saying over all the noise. The claustrophobia is overwhelming.

Next thing I know, Jaune wakes up on the floor of the bar with me still inside him. I can't shake him. Nobody notices us, or if they do, they have left Jaune alone.

Jaune stands up and announces that I must have fallen asleep. Everyone nods and smiles. "You are free to do anything here," Thierry says and offers to buy Jaune a drink. "We are in accord of who are you."

"Jaune is tired," I say. Everyone smiles and nods. Jaune can say anything and get the same reaction.

"Can we go," I whisper in Marie-Yves's ear. It's her flesh-colored Nandi and if I left on my own Jaune wouldn't know my way home. "Jaune needs to take a shower. To get this smell off of me."

Before we go back to her habitation, we stop by the studio. Marie-Y insists she has to show Jaune something. "What could be so important at this hour?" I keep asking.

"You'll see," she keeps saying. And this is where Jaune first gets to know her intimately. Right here on the floor of the editing room where I'm writing from now. Marie-Y never even gets around to showing Jaune what it is she has to show me.

Act VII: Scene vii
Jaune Awakes in the Ark Bilge (the Aftermath)

INT. Marie-Yves's Habitation Set.[96] Studio la Suture.
Morning. December 9, 2005.

I am no longer sleeping on Marie-Yves's conch couch, but in her bed.[97] Meltwater from Jaune's face wakes her, in turn waking me. "Sorry," I say. "He can't help himself." I turn on the light to check the color. It's okay. It's not blood red but milky white.

"Why is this happening?" she asks.

"I don't know. Could be the molting. It hurts whatever it is. To tell the truth, Jaune feels a bit undernourished. Or maybe he misses Troy more than I think."

I turn off the light and bury Jaune's head in what bosom she has, letting him melt all over the place. "D'accord," she keeps saying, while smoking his phalangocyte through her duckbill. "Let it harden, harder, harden, harder." Jaune releases himself and his skin is raw and fresh, if not milky with moonlight. Marie-Y's chest is glistening with Jaune, along with some molting of her own — patches of fur clinging to nubile peach fuzz.

When I suck on her nipple as an afterthought, sour milk comes out. "Arrêt!" she yells. "That is no for your special, not on this day first." I slide my head down her wet belly and that's when Jaune first discovers the tear in her furry skin. The opening where I remember John sticking his whole hand the first morning I arrived in Paris. I turn on the light and finger at the opening, verifying Jaune's suspicions. "Not there either!" she says, slapping Jaune's hand away. "Behave you now not for to be a wound." I retreat, leaving Jaune puddled in her belly button. She tastes him with the tip of her tongue. "Your sex smells special of escargot," she says.

"Maybe this is a side-effect of the molting. Or a change in diet."

"What is really happening in there?" she says, her teeth flashing from within the dark cavity formed by her porkfish lips.

---

[96] This was one of Troy's last requests—a lifesize recreation of Marie-Y's habitation. Not that there was a scene in the movie that called for it. Troy just wanted it to sleep in.

[97] A boat prop, an ark actually from *Mutiny on the Ark of Noah*.

"John and I used to go deep sea fishing as kids," I confess. Marie-Y slithers her coiled tongue through her porkfish lips to lap more of the puddled mess from her own bellybutton. "The only way our father would take us was if I promised to clean the fish we caught. John would get to go, but he wouldn't have to clean the fish because I was the one who made the promise to begin with. When we'd come back from being out at sea, our father would place a chair by the sink for me to stand on. He would dump all the dead fish from the burlap sack into the sink. Some had their eyes bulging out because we had brought them up from such great depths without letting them decompress."

"What is this all to do with why Jaune so melts comme?"

"When they'd leave me alone to clean the fish I would cry."

"Why? Did you for the fish feel sorry?"

Jaune switches off the light.

"Were it to you sad it will not go on forever? The special fishing?"

"Let's just go to bed," Jaune says. I lay his head back down on her belly. She suckles on his limp phalangocyte some more. *I cried while I lopped off the head and inserted the knife into the anus, slitting the belly open. I cried while scooping out the guts and scraping the spinal cord. As I sliced off the fins. As I scraped the scales. And when it came down to eating the fish, you can bet I wouldn't even taste what I'd caught. I didn't have a problem with eating fish in general or the ones John caught. Just the ones I caught. The idea of this used to really anger our mother. She forced me to eat some of what I'd caught and I never got over it. My brother and my dad held my arms down while our mother forked the fish into my mouth. She forced me to swallow, but the second they let go I regurgitated. I couldn't help myself. I knew this was part of being in our species, but I couldn't stomach the thought of it. We went through it all again, only this time our mother force-fed me my throw up of what I'd caught. And then I threw it up again, and they made me eat what I had regurgitated twice and so on until I passed out not knowing who I was anymore.*

Marie-Y fumbles for her cigarettes in the darkness. She lights one and I stare at the glowing ember and the silhouette of her protuberant porkfish lips. She checks the clock, then contorts herself until I'm insider her again. "Does this count yet?" she asks, exhaling into my mouth. I can taste Jaune on her breath. She twists her head around until my phalangocyte is perfectly fitted between her porkfish lips.

"Does what count?"

She unlatches her lip grip and laps up what spilled. "This ici. Even if here we are on the ground lot of studio. In this prop of bed lust."

"Jaune wouldn't know," Jaune says. "No one's written the book on this." Marie-Y degenerates into rapid breathing, hissing through clenched teeth. During these times she disgusts me, but I keep reminding myself this is what it takes to be in our species. To be special. Not to follow raw instinct but to gloss over such indignities in the name of evolution. And it's not me but Jaune that comes in her. She turns the light back on and reaches for her syringe. Thumps around on her face and sticks the needle in the crease of her deflating lips.

"Jaune thinks as a whole you're evolving," I say. "I'm not sure into what, but you are changing, and change is always good."

"To you too," she says, turning off the light and sinking back into our boat-bed. "It is a feeling part of you which is a sprout in my cave."

I fall asleep and dream that Marie-Yves and I are at a restaurant, and so is Troy. Marie-Y and Troy are a couple, though Marie-Y looks just like Élodée. Troy and what looks like Élodée are fondling each other under the table, which really pisses me off even if, on the inside, Élodée is Marie-Y. I keep telling them to, "knock it up," and every time I say this they crack up laughing.

A waitress[98] tells us the special of the day is conch cocktail. I mechanically sniff at her before Marie-Y slaps me hard and says, "this is reserved not for people that serve on you!" The waitress is distracted and blushing because of Troy and Élodée's public display of affection. She fans herself with a menu, proclaiming she is hot. I ask her what is in the conch cocktail and she says it isn't really conch, but a type of French shellfish that there is no word for in English. She is describing with her hands what sort of sea organism they put in the cocktail when she steps on my shoe and loses her balance, knocking a glass of wine on me as she falls. I impulsively reach out to grab her but instead knock over the candle that is on our table. This all happens in slow motion, the past bunching up all over the present. The waitress falls onto her back, her dress spilling up. The candlestick falls after her, spraying red molten wax all over her garter belt and exposed swollen belly. Not only is it revealed that she is pregnant, but she is wearing a wooden mask that splinters off. Underneath it, she is

---

[98] Dressed like the stereotypical French maid in the movie. See *Act I: Scene ii.*

Marie-Yves. She is in disguise so she can spy on Troy and Élodée, who by now really is Élodée. The tablecloth catches fire and we are rooted to our seats.

I was getting hotter and hotter, burning alive, until I woke up to discover it is the bed Marie-Y and I are sleeping on that is on fire. Marie-Y had fallen asleep smoking. I wake her up and pull the burning sheets off the bed, wadding them into a smoldering ball. Marie-Y runs to the bathroom naked to get a scooper full of water to douse the mattress for good measure.

When we get the flames out, she starts laughing hysterically, which causes Jaune to laugh because I'd never heard her laugh, and her laugh sounded funny, all high-pitched and wailing like a hyena.

"Why are you laughing?" Jaune asks.

"You have on special pants. Your wearing of them and the fire makes my hot crotch," she says, tapping her watch then fingering herself. "Come now release it to me sweat down here to harden harder now with me without."

Jaune is indeed wearing pants. In fact, they are Troy's leather pants he had left me. I don't remember having put them on. "A natural reflex to the fire," I say.

Act VII: Scene viii
Arrested for Waking

INT. Bernard's Habitation. Paris.
November 27, 2005. 2:30 PM

"¡Bernard!" yells Marie-Yves, pounding on his door with her first. "¡Allez!" We were supposed to be filming the scene with the porkfishes in the river Seine. Bernard had pulled some strings so we could get the porkfishes in the river for a three-hour time slot, and then didn't bother to show up himself. Not the first time he had pulled a stunt like this. And it was always Marie-Y and Jaune that had to go wake him up. The scene couldn't proceed without the director.

She knocks again and tries the door. It's open. Bernard's habitation is in complete disarray. Bernard is naked, passed out on the couch. Two Italian Greyhounds are curled up next to him.

179

It appears he has thrown up all over himself. There are wine bottles and drug paraphernalia strewn about the habitation and it smells sour and stale.

"Something has gone off in here," I announce.

"Not this again," says Marie-Y. She picks up a syringe off the coffee table and sniffs it. Jaune pries the script from Bernard's hands and plops himself in the plush chair opposite the couch. Thumbing through it, I see Bernard is rewriting the part leading up to today. Troy lives after all. I inform Marie-Y but she doesn't care. She goes into the kitchen to fetch a glass of water from the tap. She comes back and dumps the water over Bernard. The two Italian Greyhounds scatter with their tails between their legs. Usually this is when Bernard would moan and wake up, but not this time. He remains naked and motionless. He is skinny and pale with track-marks running up his arms and legs. His hunched back is covered with tufts of black hair and pimples. The water dripping off him hardens to candle wax. Marie-Y checks his pulse then makes a half-ass attempt to blow air into his mouth. I feel I should be doing something, so I pound on his chest, counting, though I don't know what I'm counting to. Nothing changes. There's just the sound of the dogs licking themselves. Marie-Y grabs his cell phone off the coffee table and dials three numbers. She gets off the phone after reporting it. "Do you want to try it, giving your mouth to his mouth?"

I eye his crooked yellow teeth. "That's where Jaune draws the line," I say. "I don't care how real this is."

On the wall is a primitive spray-painted vagina, with the scrawled words, "Mother Mary comes to me," and "get back where you belong."

"John's been here," Jaune says.

"John or Jaune?"

"Troy-John."

"How can you know?"

"I recognize his work anywhere."

"This? Is it in theory art? Or was it here before?"

"I never noticed it before."

"Maybe is it Bernard to act as Troy to act as John."

"What succession takes place off the grid?" squelches the translating talkie-talkie.

"Bernard does not display the essential signs for living," answers Marie-Yves through the talkie-talkie. "What is the statute of the ensemble on the grid? Done."

180

"The species specialist states that the porkfishes are desiccated. We must obtain them in water. A figure of authority must proclaim the decision. Done."

"The director is not in a decision of supination to grant the retrieval order. It is me by my invested will proclaiming the release of the porkfishes to the river and the subsequent retrieval. Continue to draw film while to pre-establish motion until you have of the news of us. Done."

The barking dogs announce the arrival of the paramedics. I feel a bond with them, having just acted the part of a Parisian medic. One of the medics pulls a needle loaded with epinephrine out of his bag.

"It's just like the movie," Jaune says. "This was the part I was playing. Only this time he really looks dead."

The medics work on Bernard for a while, then cover him with a sheet. "Désolé," says one of them. By this time a detective is there. These are real people that don't speak English so I have no idea what is going on. Fortunately we have our talkie-talkies so I can at least piece together Marie-Y's end of the conversation. "Afflicted?" she says to the paramedic. "It is very you make will for him?.. It is very that it is you will be enough?.. It is his death for real truth?.. Afflict my ass... Attention... Bernard makes an attempt have you rented?.. Part of his world it presents in film."

"Are these directives you give to the ensemble, done?" asks the assistant A.D in between blasts of squelching feedback.

"Be unaware of my orders," yells Marie-Y into the talkie-talkie. "I speak here to a male nurse of the city. In truth. In appearance Bernard is dead. Done."

"Bernard is dead?" asks the assistant A.D.

"Unconfirmed. The stay in accordance for the confirmation. In the mean time, you have a will to remain silent. Done."

"Qui est ce?" asks the paramedic.

"The sub-sub-director of one important and high-budget film of which we draw. There is a porkfish release in the river whose livelihood dependency on resolution our here. Without his continuation it is us that may no continue not."

The medic shrugs and hands her a card with a number for a forensic pathologist. The detective steps forward and starts in on a line of questioning directed at me.

"Let him talk into your talkie-talkie," I say. "So I can understand."

"Did it leave the letter of suicide?" the detective's voice is translated. Marie-Y says no. The detective takes the script from my hands and starts flipping through it. "I take this as proof."

"This is the receipt!" says Marie-Y through the talkie-talkie for my benefit. "It is how we carry on knowledge to make film. Without this receipt we know not how to carry on living."

The detective puts the screenplay in a bag and writes the word "preuve" on it. Next thing I know he is rifling through my pockets. "Hey!" I say, "what is this?"

"You must let him feel for you," says Marie-Y.

"He's grabbing my balls!"

The detective pulls a pen and a wad of papers out of my pocket. "Qu'est-ce que c'est?"

"A personal letter from my brother." Marie-Y's talkie-talkie translates my voice to French. "And a newspaper clipping."

"Pourquoi?"

"Why? Because he sent it to me. There's the envelope with the postmark if you don't believe me. What does this have to do with anything?"

"It is we who are in discovery of the body," says Marie-Y. "In France the discovery of spoken body says you are capable of spoken death."

"À qui ce souci?" asks the detective, attempting to read the newspaper clipping.

"It's about a fire," I say, "in a pond back home. It doesn't have to do with any of this."

"Et ceci?" the detective asks, unfolding some more papers from my pocket.

"It's an autopsy report. Of our mother."

"This is your mother?" asks the detective through the talkie-talkie. "Why is it you carry this proper on your own corpse?"

"That's my business."

"The affairs of your named so mother is my affair."

"It's research. For this book I'm writing."

"It will be taken in consideration to accord you a pardon."

"A pardon? For what?"

"You know what it is you did already in your mind. Your guilt will put in a frame who you are." The detective puts the pond fire newspaper clipping, our mother's autopsy report and the letter from John into separate plastic bags and labels them as evidence. "You must have direction for your remains to be silent," he says. "Your words are a will to be employed against yourself in an arena of law. It is your right to have a presence during your own interrogation…"

"I can't believe this is happening!" I say. "Are we being arrested? For real? Is this permanent?"

"In France, it is true," says Marie-Y. "You are guilty until there is proof you are innocent. It is we who must provide for our own innocence in the form of evidence."

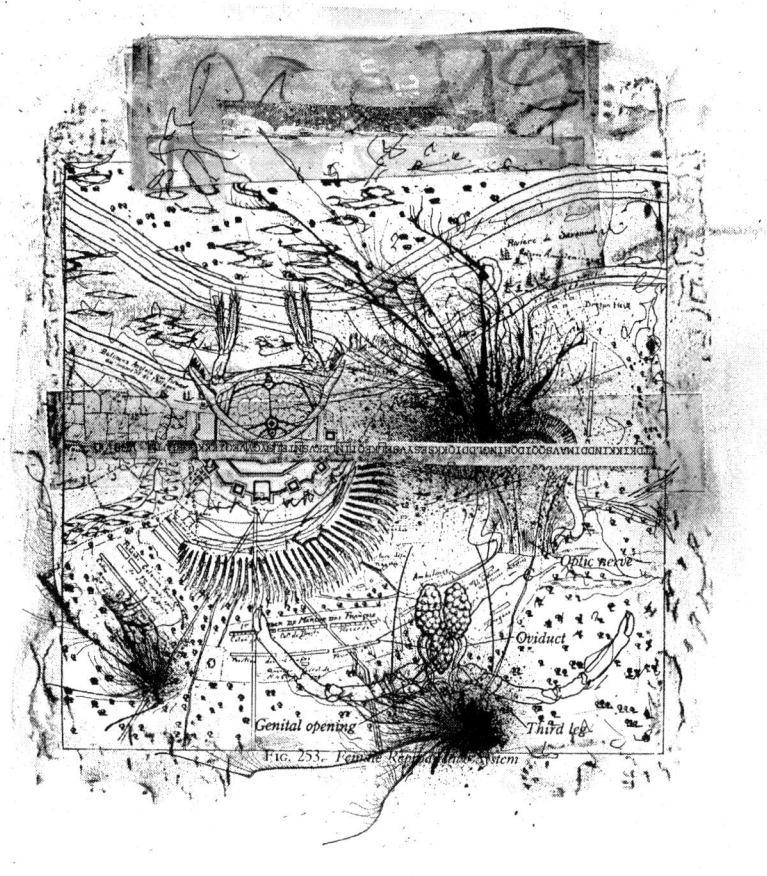

FIG. 253. *Female Reproductive System*

Gaston Containment Pond Catches Fire

SAVANNAH, GA, November 28, 2005 — Fireman are still puzzling over yesterday's mysterious fire at the Gaston Sewage Treatment Center on the outskirts of Savannah. At 8:40 AM they responded to multiple calls of a mysterious smelling smoke. The smoke appeared to be coming from the Gaston Sewage Treatment center, but since the facility has not been in use for some time, the access road was overgrown and they were not able to get the fire trucks through. When the firemen eventually were able to penetrate the dense bush and cut through the rusty fence (and evidently fend off a pack of feral dogs), they discovered the pond itself was on fire. Since the pond was surrounding by a wide barrier of clay, the fire didn't pose any danger of spreading. One fireman contracted rabies from a dog bite sustained fighting the fire, otherwise no other injuries were reported.

Helicopters were able to bring in buckets scooped from Mary X. Lake to quench the blaze, but it still remains smoldering.

Fire Captain Jake Bernadahl stated that the fire was 99.99% contained, though admitted the cause of the fire was a mystery. "[A fire] needs fuel, and at this time we have not been able to identify the source that has been feeding the fire."

As for a source of ignition, no lightning strikes have been reported in the area for the past week. Rumors were circulating that it was neighborhood pranksters, a hidden oil well, or some even went as far as to speculate that it was an emergent volcano. The leading theory at this point, according to Capt. Bernadahl, was that the suns rays were magnified through a piece of broken glass, generating enough heat to start the fire. "[Local kids] must have broken a bottle or were playing with fireworks." Though this doesn't answer the question of what is actually doing the burning. Other evidence gathered from the scene included a milk jug with remnants of what appeared to be blood, an apparent movie script (entitled "shooting script") riddled with bullet holes and a video camera whose contents were not released to the public or media as the case is still under investigation.

Calvin White, a local surveyor who was not only responsible for surveying the site, but also surveying and naming Mary X. Lake, stated that as recently as May 2002, when he went to reoccupy the site, the boundaries of the containment pond were still intact, though he said he would not be surprised if it has dried up in recent years. "It could have been a buildup of organic matter, like a compost heap. Under ideal conditions of pressure, heat, and with all this decaying matter and sludge, it could possibly undergo combustion."

Studio Arrest

EXT. Marie-Yves Habitation Set, Studio la Suture.
Day. December 10, 2005.

This business around Bernard's death has thrown a wrench into this movie reel. The first order of business was to have us transferred to the Studio la Suture jail and tried within the confines of the studio court, who operated under their own jurisdiction. According to the actor playing the lawyer assigned to me, I possessed "artistic immunity," combined with a "god-given right to practice suspension of belief." Marie-Yves and I were released on "our own recognizance" and put under "studio arrest" so we could finish the film. Footage from our actual trial was incorporated into the actual film. Upon release, Marie-Y and I were both assigned as "co-Acting-Directors," the studio court's logic being that we were the ones that had discovered the corpse.

During the trial and our studio arrest, we never returned to Marie-Y's real habitation. We lived on the set 24/7. Since we were free and back together (within the confines of the studio), Marie-Y decided to have an intrauterine device implanted in her. Ten years of tricking her body into thinking she was pregnant had wreaked havoc on her psyche, so she had gone off the pill. After the IUD was implanted, she started to feel a gnawing pain in her uterus. Her Ob/Gyn (in the film) said this was natural, that a "wandering womb," was a common side effect.

During our studio arrest I was asked to rewrite the script according to Bernard's last wishes. Even though I had only skimmed it briefly before it was confiscated as evidence, I was the only one (from the studio) that had laid eyes on his final version of the script. Marie-Y was of no help during this period. She had used up her allotted five sick days the studio granted her and was now into her unpaid leave. All she did was sleep in our bedroom set on the studio grounds, with the entire crew watching. Even my rewriting of the script was being filmed, which was something I had apparently scripted in the rewritten script.

"The pain is subsistent," says Marie-Y, both in reality and subsequently in the script. "But in still I not do feel normal no."

                    JAUNE
        You have been on the pill so many years
        you don't know what normal is.

Marie-Y's function as continuity had been neglected due to her
hiatus and newfound co-acting-directorial responsibilities. The
movie was becoming more and more discontinuous. When Marie-
Y woke up nauseous a few mornings later, I was in part relieved
at the simplicity of the diagnosis.

                    JAUNE
        You know what this means?

                                            Cut to:

Marie-Y hunched over the toilet. She produces a gun[99]
from her pant lining and pulls the trigger. A red
flag shooting from the tip of the barrel screams
"BANG!" just like in the cartoons, causing Jaune to
burst out laughing.

                    JAUNE
        Where did you find this?

                    MARIE-YVES
        The   doctors   me   put   to   this,   crazy,
        right?

                    JAUNE
        The doctor-actors from the studio?

                    MARIE-YVES
        What other doctor-type is there?

                    JAUNE
        Are you saying we should have the baby?

                    MARIE-YVES
        Pregnant   was   I   before,   but   the   IUD
        inside planted it fucked me with, my
        lining of uterus. This is fucked part!
        This is my rejecting.

Montage sequence:
- Marie-Y being restless and irritable, punctuated by
an occasional burst of hysterical laughter.
- Jaune tells her to come to bed.

---

[99] Even though in reality she never allowed guns in her habitation.

186

- Marie-Y's health deteriorates. Her hair becomes coarse and matted. She doesn't bother wearing pants.
- Jaune directs Marie-Y to act restless and decrepit.
- Marie-Y complains of pain but refuses care.
- Jaune consults the script and tells her again to come to bed.
- Marie-Y becomes increasingly bloated, more hunched.
- Marie-Y paces back and forth in the darkness.

                                                    Cut to:

Marie-Y throws a pillow at Jaune.

                    MARIE-YVES
          What is it you look at? I no to be type
          animal not!

                    JAUNE
          Just come to bed.

                    MARIE-YVES
          You   are   some   part   of   it!   The
          conspiration.

                    JAUNE
          Cut! Check the gate.

Marie-Y strips off her porkfish bill. "This is a cause of hurt for me," she says throwing the prosthetic bill to the floor. "Do I need keep to wear this?"

"It's a wrap," I say removing my own prosthetic phalangocyte, "we're done for the day." Élodée comes to my aid but I wave her off and peel away the excess mounting glue on my own. I return to the other side of the camera to sit in the chair with "Jaune" written on it. Marie-Y dives into the bed of her habitation set and remains laying face down. The Director of Photography lights a cigarette and migrates towards the Kraft table where the others have congregated, sniffing and rubbing each other up. The Assistant Director of Photography starts to remove the film cartridge before I stop him. I motion for him to roll the film again. Marie-Y remains motionless, face down. The Assistant D.P. keeps looking to me and I motion to keep it rolling. Finally I motion for him to step away from behind the camera to join the D.P. at the Kraft table. I make a note of it in my logbook so I know to account for it later.

And now I'm reading it, along with notes from the studio court stenographer, taking it all into account. I also wrote that I was filming this scene to verify my suspicions: that Marie-Y did nothing but sleep when she believed the cameras weren't on her, noting in particular that, "Marie-Y needs her meds." Even with the raise I gave myself when I became co-Acting-Director, the bottom line is we're paid in stitches here, which are useless for buying anything outside of the studio. We're stuck with what's available on the studio grounds, and all the medicine here is placebo. Marie-Y lifts her head, and seeing the red light that signifies the camera is rolling, throws her pillow across the set.

"What is it you look at? I no to be type animal not."

I turn off the camera and withdraw to the conch-couch of her habitation set. Even though we are in the studio, it is physically the same conch-couch I slept on my first days in Paris, in Marie-Y's real habitation, back when I was Stu. Marie-Y falls asleep and I turn the camera back on, sneaking into bed with her. I palm her belly that is bulging and shifting before my eyes. She moans, but keeps sleeping. I finger her loose flap. Peeling it back, I reveal the pouch I had suspected was there all along.

                                                        Close up on:

Marie-Y's moist furry cavity before she wakes up and slaps Jaune's hand away.

                          JAUNE
            You've got a pouch. This isn't supposed
            to happen.

                        MARIE-YVES
                  (pulling blanket over her)
            Let me to be sleeping.

The set dresser adjusts the wrinkled sheet beneath them as they (we) are filming, tucking the sheet under Marie-Y's chin.

                          JAUNE
            Hey, a little privacy here!

                                                        Pan out:

Stagehands and extras continue to mill about.

                    JAUNE [VOICE-OVER]
No one understands me ... It doesn't
help that the battery has died on my
translating   talkie-talkie   ...
Watching Marie-Yves sleep, I question
the truth of what I witnessed ...
Maybe I was dreaming? ... I can't
check on her pouch because she's
rolled over with the blanket clutched
to her belly.

                                              Zoom in on:

Matted fur of her pubic region.

                                              Pan out to:

Fur spreading around to her tailbone.

                                              Cut to:

Jaune gets up to boil eggs in the kitchen set. The
steady-cam operator steps into the frame to capture a
close-up of the cooking (within the shot).

                    JAUNE [VOICE-OVER]
A watched pot never boils ... Staring
at the eggs is when it occurred to me
that Marie-Yves never wore a purse.

                    MARIE-YVES
          ¡Coupe! Vérifiez la portè.

Marie-Yves throws the sheet off and puts on pants, but no shirt.
Barks orders through her talkie talkie. The Assistant D.P. checks
the gate. The crew smells and rubs against each other.

"Do you still want these eggs?" I ask.

"I now would want to waste not my egg appetite in the name
of a film," she says.

I crack open the eggs and spoon them onto a plate. This
whole time I assumed the folding kitchen table wasn't functional,
so I half-surprised myself when I was able to unhinge and fold it
down. There are still remnants of Marie-Y's previous sexual acts
with John,[100] even though these took place in her real habitation.
Marie-Y sits with her breasts perched on the edge of the table.

---

[100] See page 55.

While she eats her eggs in silence, I get out pen and paper to storyboard the next scene.

"How long have you known?" I ask.

"Known of what?"

"That you were part marsupial?"

"For the record?"

"Just out of curiosity," I say, putting down my pen.

Two ant-size fetuses crawl up her left breast, suckling up to her nipple. She flushes red in embarrassment, but keeps eating.

"You're a mother to boot!" I say.

"Stop please at me not to look that way. This is one half your doing."

"Half of me or half of Troy?"

"One half you, one half John."

"Can Jaune touch it?"

"Not yet. These have a weak diplomacy of immunity."

The fetuses fumble around, pawing at the air and her nipple. One of them eats the other one right before my eyes.

"Stop him!" I say.

"It's okay," says Marie-Y. "This is a natural. That is, was, fragile a runt." The one that had eaten the runt was now twice the size. It was big enough now that I could pet it with one finger and Marie-Y didn't mind.

"What should we name it?"

"This is no brains," says Marie-Y.

"John?"

Montage Sequence:

- Jaune crawls into marsupial pouch. [reverse engineered birth canal with surgical micro-cam]
- Jaune finds himself lounging in our dungeness mother.

                    JAUNE
          We need a boat. It doesn't need to be a
          real one.

- A boat appears but Jaune's twin destroys it with an axe.
- Jaune lights the remains of the boat on fire.
- Close on irritated fallopian tubes.
- Whale expels them back into the sea.

                    JAUNE
          It's only for the time being.

Autopsy Report/Ratio[99]

Name: Mary Xavier White)   Case # 1727   )
Date of Birth: April 2, 1937)   Race: White   )
Date of Autopsy: December 11, 2005)   Sex: Femail   )

Abstraction:

(A femail of adult (humane ███████ ████████ demonstrating genetic
bounds within fish) was fond discovered in the river Seine. The autopsy
herein determines the inconclusive cause of death to be ████████[100].)

Events as Unfolded:

(On 9 December 2005, ████████ rechords, an em-urgency call was
made @ a proximate 05h40m, by the $\sum$son of the belate, *John White* (a
parent a dismember of a Studio la ·Suture cinematique crew drawing in
scene on the banq of the Seine-river). Suture mail nurses (fore medics)
arrive on the scene at 05h48m. ████ describe the deceased, *Mary X.
White*, as supine, halfed (laterally) in the water, ████████ gurgling
sounds. ████████ certain in itial conditions (there were acting male
nurses on the sene of apparent in the film actual), Mary X. was of
immediate in-tubated. Due to implications in her mouthal struqure (her
lips hardened into a "bill"), an incition in her trachaea was ████████
intubation.

After the internogation, ███ indicates it that in spite of his
report/ratio, the discovery by her $\sum$son was apparently purely
coïncidente and de spite of ███████ physical anomalies de facto it was
not a member of the cast unit. D'according to $\sum$son, it had missed

---

[99] The autopsy being necessary to grant the pardon.
[100] The autopsy itself, by definition, negates all substantial facts of the living state.

being since April 1971 when ████████████████ sceen on a boat of casino proportions in addition to coast of Georgia, the United States.

During its sequent ressuscitation, it received 5 x magnesium of the epinephrine (1 via ET tubes and 4 via IV), dopamine and 7 defibrillations, which are known to induct the factitious changes of the electrolytes of blood ███████ substantiates. ████████ John White discoverer of said body, ██████████ wish to identify the body subsequently ████████████████ had died, citing the indeterminancy of quantum (proofen by cavity radiation). The identification and corrobaration genetique placed the probability of a direct genetic relation between the White of Mary X White and John as 99.9999 ± 0.0003%.

External examination:

(The corpse is that of a has well-developed, well-nurtured caucasian woman pearing the offered age of 34 (at time of death). The bodie measures 1.85 meters and gross weight 84 kilograms. The unembalmed body is well-preservatived despite carryforwards of being missing since April 1971. Rigor mortis is fully developed in muscular groups. The skin (████████ akin to fur) is intact and shows no signal of trauma. No punctures or penetration points.

Below the waist, the skin has a scaly appearance of undetermined causation. The hair is brown and 18 inches in length. The irides are hazel. The natural toothes are in good condision. Lips are hard into a bill struquce akin to a soft-bille duck or porpiose. The oral mucosa and tongue are free of in-sult or in-jury. Earlobe creases are notably absent.

The fingernails are long and clean. The fingers are partial webbed ████████████ four on each hand. Spurs emitting venom were discovered symmetrically on each hand. In lieu of feet is a dorsal aileron from what has been identified ████████ a monkfish (*Lophius*).

The neque and shouldiers and chest are symmetrical and free of scars or evident of in-jury. The breasts are unremarkable. The back is symmetrical and grossly unremarkable. The ribs assemble a boat hole (lab report indicates abnormal high wood cellulose deposiums and abnormal low calcite deposiums). Th lower extremities are symmetrical goal fused together ███████ above knees. There is only one excit hole ███████ not be determined yew this excite was for the digestive, urinary or reproductive leaflets (see *internal findings*).

An incision was discovered on the abdomomain.

No trauma was noted one the superfisial pyshical exam.

Clothing:

Not present.

Tattoos:

A siren on a flowerbed across the lower back (visible under UV light).)
* See *last page* .

Internal Examination:

(Degenerative deltas are noted in the acromiclavicular joints, knees, feet and pelvis. Calculi are persistent in urinary tract. The mucsles of the chest and abominable wall are grossly unremarkable. The peritoneal cavity is unremarkable and dry. The organs ███████ an-atomic relations, ██████ the digestif, urinary and reproduction tracts empty into a commun chamber terminating in a single excit wound. An abscess of gills of amfibious origin are presence in the lungs. The sternum and ribs are holey unremarkable.

The contents of the belly include crawdads, crabs and other sea orangisms including coelacanth (considered a long-time extinct). The presence of these arthropodic creatures ███████ imply ingestion, ██████ possible be a resulting of parasitism post-mortem.

The containment of the womb includes 348 eggs and a vestigial foetus in a stopgap of development arrest.

The heart was anatomically correct and grossly unremarkable with out any sector of recent or remote myocardial infraction.

Blood results re-vealed a grotesquely high density of red blood cells.

Neuropathology report indicates the brain is grossly unremarkable.

Toxicology reports revealed the presents of foreign anti-bodies of an unknown origin. It is advisable to note ███████ drugs/toxins ███ ███ detected by hopital toxicology testing are possible.

The individual is negative for any disease-associated mutation.   }

Autopsy Findings:

1. Blood and froth liquid peresence in lungs.
2. Well-cured suprapuic scar.
3. Fine sand particules peresence in lower respiratory passages, ███████ death by drowning. Being submerged in water secondary ██████ the primary event, ██████ sustained given the extreme nature ██████ physiological changes.
4. Presence of parasitic crabs and fish.
5. Reduced blood carbon dioxide levels indicate loss of the conscience (LOC) or "underwater blackout".

Synopsis:

(While certain grotesque abnormalities were found, causation of death remains unknown. Results are inconclusive.

The 34· year sur vival of Mary X. White d'according to her disappearance at sea █████ consequences in the creation of a bulky number of documents, ██████████ lost or discarted over the years. If is the policy of this studio that no case is never closed and that all determinations are to be reconsidered upon reciept of in-credible new information.   }

Élodée Rouge
Coroner/Make-up Artist

Suspended in Consummation

EXT. Day. River Seine, Paris.
December 13, 2005.

Troy floats naked, face down in the river. A boat
with the FILM CREW follows after him in his wake.

Close up on:

A transparent tube leading from Troy's mouth, behind
his ear and to the surface.

Cut to:

DIVER with underwater camera filming Troy from
beneath the surface.

Cut to:

Troy staring down into the murky shadows.

> TROY (VOICE-OVER)
> *It happens like it's an inevitable part
> of the script. This will be the death
> of Troy: a death by drowning. I am
> carried by this river to the sea...*

The above water camera follows his floating corpse
down the river, then pans up to the Notre Dame and
sweeps across the Paris skyline.

> TROY (V.O.)
> *Later, I will witness this as others
> see me. In the warmth of a screening
> room or theatre. Maybe this isn't the
> ending Bernard scripted, but he's dead
> now, so there's no telling. Marie-Yves
> and I are in charge. We are the only
> ones that can dictate truth. And now
> the truth is dying with me...*

Zoom in to:

Snorkeling tube. P.O.V. spirals through tube,
eventually into Troy's lungs, zooming down to the
molecular level.

TROY (V.O.)

You won't be able to see the snorkel.
It'll appear as if I'm dead. Until then
my frame of reference is unique and
real. [BEAT] It's cold and raining
above the surface. The surface of the
river that reveals the sum of the
weight beneath. I remind myself of the
eight hundred stitches a day hazard pay
I am getting and try to forget about
the here and now.

Cut to:

Film crew on boat following on the heels of Troy's floating corpse.

MARIE-YVES CURIE AS DIRECTOR
¡Plus de leaves! ·

The SET DRESSER scatters leaves into the view of the camera. He picks a live rat up by its tail and places it on Troy's back.

TROY (V.O.)

Through the white noise current of this
river, I can hear Marie-Yves' muffled
voice directing me to float naturally.
I can feel the trained rat crawling on
my back. A cold enfolding comfort is
enveloping me. I'll admit, I'm afraid
of falling asleep and dying for real.
The thought surfaces in my mind. The
temperature of this muddied water is
real. It is hard to suppress the
shivers that will give my life away...

Zoom in on:

Surface of water. Bugs and microscopic organisms suspended in cloudy amber. Again, down to molecular level, blood platelets coagulating, etc.

JAUNE (V.O)

In the comfort of your movie theatre or
home, I hope you can appreciate what
I'm going through. This is how it feels
to be Troy. This is what I needed to
know, only to find out it was all a
lie. Marie-Yves was right. I can still
smell her cheese-reeking sweat and her
diabetic breath. Even in death, I can

196

*taste the fondue and the mulchy taste
of wine. Her tongue was a clammy fish
darting in and out of my mouth...*

Cut to:

Troy's open mouth in the murky water, his swollen
tongue hanging in the open. Pan out of water to
Troy's naked corpse floating under a bridge. P.O.V.
bobbers above and below the surface of the river.

JAUNE AS TROY (V.O.)
*We floated for an eternity. It was too
late to turn back. We'd gone past the
point of no return. I pretended to do
everything Troy did, but I couldn't
pretend to do this.*

Close up on:
Full frontal penetration.

Zoom out, revealing:

Jaune on top of Marie-Yves, fucking her, but it's
more like two bodies colliding over and over,
tangled, unable to separate. Marie-Y pushes Jaune off
her and lurches onto the floor, crawling for the
bathroom.

JAUNE
(in Troy's delirious voice)
What's happening here?

Cut to:

Jaune's cock jerking and shriveling. Marie-Y vomits
before she reaches the toilet.

JAUNE AS TROY (V.O.)
*I can still see her now, underwater. In
the moonlit darkness I can make out her
white bony back, her marsupial pouch
and the furry beginnings of a tail as
she scampers across the carpet. It
hasn't been that long since we crawled
out of the ocean. I can hear Marie-
Yves' external voice directing us to
cut, but I am not ready to surface. I
have graduated from being John's stand-
in, to being Troy's double, to being
his understudy... and now to this. I'm*

> *mixed up with John and Troy to the*
> *point that we are indistinguishable.*
> *All our seeds are blended up inside*
> *Marie-Yves. I can't live with this.*
> *Even if this is in the script...*

                                        Flash on:

Two intertwined crayfish, claws locked, tails thrusting. White corpuscular globules scattering in the open water.

              JAUNE AS TROY (V.O.)
> *The only thing we were guilty of was*
> *trying to make sense of him. We knew*
> *going into it that we'd inherently kill*
> *him by trying to make sense of Troy.*

Underwater camera travels through sewage pipes and surfaces, revealing the inside of a toilet. Marie-Yves is hunched over it. A cola broth with white fish and gummy bear chunks gushes from her mouth. She convulses again in a bout of dry heaves. Her white amphibious skin is stretched taut over the curvature of her spine.

              JAUNE AS TROY (V.O.)
She is fully realized. Her fur has molted completely.

              MARIE-YVES AS DIRECTOR
                (via the translating
                   talkie-talkie)
Cut! Verify the slit.

Jaune (acting as Troy) remains motionless, floating spread-eagle, his limp shriveled penis dangling underwater. Bubbles issue from his mouth as he begins to sink.

              JAUNE AS TROY (V.O.)
> *I'm below the surface looking up at the*
> *casino boat, at our mother and father*
> *gambling. I see our mother come lean*
> *over the rail, peering down.*

                                        Cut to:

MARY X. WHITE leaning over the rail. Her eyes close, the p.o.v. spins, falling.

                    JAUNE AS TROY (V.O.)
        I can't tell if she notices me beneath
        the surface. She looks preoccupied. She
        throws up...
                                            Cut to:

Fishes flocking from the shadows to devour her vomit
in a feeding frenzy. Porkfishes swoop in to in turn
devour the fish.
                                        Zoom in on:

Porkfish morphing into a mermaid with the torso of
Marie-Y. Jaune latches on to her in an underwater
embrace.

                    JAUNE AS TROY (V.O.)
        The white noise of the river drowns out
        the rush of blood running through my
        own veins. I relish in the serenity
        coming from a fleeting act that others
        will mistake as real.

                        MARIE-YVES
                    (via the translating
                        talkie-talkie)
        Cut! It's a wrap.

Jaune, still acting as Troy, remains floating on the
river.

                    JAUNE AS STU (V.O.)
                    (in southern accent)
        When I open my eyes, our mother is no
        longer at the rail of the boat. Instead,
        our father is standing there with a gun.
        He is fixing to shoot the gun into the
        ocean where I am, though he apparently
        can't see me. He closes his eyes and
        empties his gun into the water.

                        DECKHAND
        What the hell do you think you're
        doing?

                        OUR FATHER
        Fishing.

                        STU (V.O.)
        By seeing what floats to the surface,
        our father could deduce what lived in
        the depths.

                            199

<pre>
                    MARIE-YVES
                 (yelling, without
                 a talkie-talkie)
        It is a wrap!
</pre>

Jaune remains floating.

<pre>
                    MARIE-YVES
        Jaune! It is time for you to cut.
</pre>

The concerned crew gathers at the edge of the boat.

<pre>
                    MARIE-YVES
        Troy?!
</pre>

Troy remains motionless.

<pre>
                    MARIE-YVES
        John?!
</pre>

The boom mic operator prods John with his boom.

<pre>
                    MARIE-YVES
        Stu?!
</pre>

No response from Stu.

<pre>
                    MARIE-YVES
        Derek?!
</pre>

Derek responds, pulling himself out of the water onto the camera boat. The crew lets out a collective sigh of relief. Marie-Y hands me a large white towel.

<pre>
                    MARIE-YVES
        You did it! We are wrapped.
</pre>

Marie-Y throws her dog-eared script up into the air. I'm wrapped in the white towel, shivering.

<pre>
                    MARIE-YVES
        It is now behind us.
</pre>

The pages scatter in the wind and settle in our wake.

Savannah, Georgia—New York City

1997—2008